THE AUTHOR

Nick Cann was born in London ir
Since 1981 he has worked as a m;
newspaper and book designer.
In 1989 he moved to Northern Ir
where he works as a journalist and ....
design consultant.
On the Island is his second published novel,
his first, *Jake's Eulogy,* was published in 2005.

ON THE ISLAND

BY NICK CANN

indiego.co.uk

FIRST PUBLISHED IN THE UK IN 2009 BY

indiego

HOLYWOOD, COUNTY DOWN

© indiego 2009

TEXT © NICK CANN

ALL RIGHTS RESERVED

Nick Cann is hereby identified as author of this work in accordance with
section 77 of the copyright, designs & patents act 1988

ISBN 0-9549066-1-6

WRITTEN BY NICK CANN

PROOF-READING: JANE HARRISON

FRONT COVER PHOTO: KHARA PRINGLE
(DROP IN OF ICE CREAM: ROMAS FOORD)

PRINTED BY GRANGE PRINTING

All rights reserved.
No part of this publication may be reproduced, stored in a retrieval system or transmitted
in any form or by any means – nor by way of trade or otherwise, be lent, resold, hired out
or otherwise circulated – in any form binding or cover other than that in which it is
published and without the publisher's prior permission in writing and without similar
condition, including this condition being imposed on the subsequent purchaser.

FOR JAMES KEALY

WITH SPECIAL THANKS TO:
My wife, Dawn
Parents, Brian & Sheila
Daughters, Sophie & Chloe and my sisters, Wendy & Judy
also my faithful dog, Jo

ACKNOWLEDGMENTS:
My father, Brian Cann, who proof-read and advised, but sadly passed away
just three months before this book went to press

Also: Ray Reihill, Stuart Young, Neil Hughes & Billy McCandless for their advice
Ellen and Damien Morelli of Morelli's Portstewart for allowing me use of
the 'Nuts Galore' brand name (my favourite ice cream)
Martin Casey and the regulars at the Harbour Bar, Sheephaven Bay

1

4.00am, Friday 22nd April, 1994. Belfast.

Thomas Eugene McShane's eye still hadn't recovered from the pruning of his mother's privet the previous summer. Gardening was a chore he could be doing without, but it had to be done. He'd finished trimming the hedge and was pulling away the cuttings when he yanked one into his face, giving real meaning to the saying: 'Better than a poke in the eye with a sharp stick'.

It was a minor injury, but the soreness was mighty. God it hurt! With time it healed, then rarely bothered him; until out of the blue the pain would suddenly return, like this morning. It was there when he awoke and he could barely force the bastard open; it was as if the upper lid was glued down. Tight shut. Strange. For months, nothing, and then this. Glued-down-eye.

McShane lay in bed, his good eye, the left one, staring across at the window waiting for the dawn light to amble through the blind. But it wasn't coming. Not yet. *Bloody insomnia,* he thought. Time was when McShane would put his head down and could be guaranteed sleep for eight hours. Quality sleep. Pure gold. A great knack. He could sleep anywhere, day or night, even standing up, but not now. Now he heard his wife coming in; the front door slammed behind her.

Drunk again. It must be four or five, he thought.

McShane couldn't be sure whether the slamming of the door was designed to wake him up. A malicious act, but then it was easy for him to be paranoid. Recently, paranoia had set in with the vigour of rust.

He could hear drink in his wife's footsteps as she stumbled on the stairs. He braced himself for her arrival – tracing her progress across the landing in her bumps and scrapes. A pause and then the anticipation of her entry into his room. But she didn't come in this time; the door of the spare bedroom swung shut with a thump. They'd had separate rooms for some time now.

McShane had left his door open though. A signal of sorts. On this occasion however, she either didn't or couldn't read the sign or was just too pissed to care. He was cursed with a man's appetite for sex, but she wasn't as hungry as he tonight. Perhaps not as hungry as the last time she'd taken up his subtle invitation. But that was over a month ago, it was hard to be accurate, and the marriage had deteriorated further since. Then he'd left the bedroom door open and lain awake waiting for her to return from whichever city centre bar she had graced. Of course, she came home drunk as usual and, for once, wandered into his room to say goodnight. She sat on the bed and stroked his brow.

They both knew what this meant and before long they were kissing; long open-mouthed kisses with lips pressing hard. Sex would be a certainty now, he knew. She flopped down onto the bed already semi-undressed. The rest of her clothes were pulled off with urgency, and then she was on him; thrusting her hips into his loins until he was inside her. But he exploded too soon, groaning at the exquisite burst of energy that seemed to suck him further into her, but guilty that he was spent when she was yet to come, and would want to. He was shrinking away from her fast and drained of the vital spark that had inspired the act in the first place. The guilt killed off any sense of satisfaction. She rolled off him and slept, her deep breathing building into a drunken snore. McShane rolled the other way and stared at the window. Like now. Stared at the window and waited for the dawn.

The separation was dragging on, but a settlement would be coming soon, and then divorce and then their release. He would have moved out of the house weeks ago, but his solicitor had cautioned against it. "Bad for your negotiating position," she advised. For most solicitors divorce is business. For him it was major surgery. An amputation. No, the word 'separation' was right. This was like the separating of conjoined twins; for they couldn't live together – with time, one would kill the other – but then the operation was also as likely to kill them as cure them.

McShane had hoped for a cure. None had come. He'd had enough and wanted it over – and now. Sod the negotiations. Sod the 'who gets what'; there was nothing to have anyway.

That they didn't have kids was a blessing and would make the split easier, but it was also a regret. What did they have to show for their ten years of hard labour? Fading memories of their initial romance and the ensuing nights of passion, a box of holiday photos and a collection of junk that wouldn't fetch a fiver in a car boot sale.

McShane turned over and attempted to sleep again. Too hot and restless, he shut his eyes and tried some mental arithmetic; running through the maths of the divorce settlement again in his head. But he couldn't get anywhere with it; couldn't concentrate – couldn't remember the detail.

Then he tensed when he saw the faces. He knew the faces well. They were a familiar apparition. They came to haunt him regularly now, either in the middle of the night or in the early morning. There was a crowd of them. Always seven and the same seven – and always in the bedroom window, pressed tight to the glass looking in: four men, two women and a small child, all staring in at him from outside. The adults would smile at him, warm friendly smiles; they almost looked saintly.

The child was the ghost of Colin Downey, aged ten. That had been a terrible mistake, his worst. A stray bullet, a ricochet. It had almost got McShane shot too. His side didn't tolerate mistakes.

The rest of the ghosts, he couldn't remember their names, were people he had eliminated with impunity and for whose deaths he had been congratulated by his comrades; they had encouraged him to be proud of his work, and so he had been. But not now. And now his victims wouldn't let him sleep. And they always smiled – smiled with broad innocent grins.

Each face was decorated with a red dot; a 7.62 millimetre bullet hole which sat on the forehead like a Hindu marking – bang in the centre, just above the bridge of the nose. Each had been a clean job. Just one shot. Except for the child. The apparition of Colin Downey stared back through its one good eye, the face made grotesque by the gaping hole where the other should have been and where blood now oozed in the socket. A fatal error, McShane had missed his target. And unlike his companion ghosts, the child ghost never smiled.

McShane would have screamed, but couldn't. He had been trained to keep quiet, knew that to draw any attention to himself could mean death or capture; for 'they' were listening. Listening out for people like him. Everywhere they were listening for clues. McShane pulled a pillow over his face and thought of his wife and what he would do to her new man if he met him.

2

5.00am, Friday 22nd April, 1994. The Port of Rotterdam.

"Waltzing Matilda, Waltzing Matilda,
Who'll come a-waltzing Matilda with me?"

An Australian song, a Dutch accent. Captain Jan Vogel stared into the mist from the bridge of the *Contessa Rose*. His voice was so low, so gravelly, that the song sounded more like a prayer.

Holding binoculars up to his face had caused the blood to drain from his hands so that the fingers were starting to feel the first tinge of a cramp. The glasses were lowered; the merchant vessel could navigate itself through the fog anyway, as the blips and bleeps from the on-board computer reminded him.

Captain Vogel could make the crossing to Ireland with his eyes shut in almost any conditions however, with or without satellite navigation. Rotterdam – Belfast, Belfast – Rotterdam, Rotterdam – Belfast. Same route, same ship, same cargo. Colombian house coal bound for Northern Ireland.

Why the hell are there no coal mines in Northern Ireland? he mused. *What the hell happened to British coal?*

The crossing would be calm, but sliding out of the harbour the captain would have been happier to swap the sea mist ahead for the blue sky over the Dutch coast behind. And today the crossing would be slow.

Captain Vogel leaned forward, pressing his face against the cold glass to peer the length of the deck below; a final check before the ship's bows were enveloped in fog.

Ship? It disturbed Captain Vogel to think of this metal hulk as a ship. His definition demanded sails and rigging, masts and booms, gunwales and decking, wood and canvas. Ships were female, graceful and pervaded with the scent of tar, salt water and seaweed. The *Contessa Rose* smelt of diesel, was hard and brutal and rusting. A female impersonator caked with a mask of white paint in a vain attempt to disguise the ravages of a hard life at sea. The journey to Belfast could be cruel in winter.

> *"Waltzing Matilda, Waltzing Matilda,*
> *Who'll come a-waltzing Matilda with me?"*

Silence.

Rotterdam – Belfast, Belfast – Rotterdam. Same route, same ship, same cargo. But not on this trip, a maiden voyage of a kind. Who would suspect that the *Contessa Rose* might be carrying contraband into Ireland? Not Captain Vogel, not the shipping company and not Her Majesty's Customs in the Port of Belfast. Or so the recipients in Northern Ireland hoped. Their arrogance encouraged them to believe that Customs officers could be bribed or intimidated should they pose a threat.

Unknown to Captain Vogel therefore, shortly after their arrival, two industrial-strength bin liners will be carried ashore – rubbish bags to the innocent eye. In each bag will be another valuable export from Colombia: 25 pounds of white powder, packaged and ready for market. As arranged, the bags will be deposited in a skip. And then the risk: left overnight before the skip is collected in the morning by lorry, then the bags retrieved by a stooge at the city dump and, finally, delivered safe into the hands of the importer – a paramilitary warlord. Easy. Easy money. The first of many such deliveries to follow along this route. For whence came arms, will now come narcotics.

Captain Vogel sounded the ship's horn as the *Contessa Rose* glided into the main channel. He hoped there would be enough visibility mid-crossing to take out his five-wood and knock a few golf balls down the deck once out of view of the harbour.

3

McShane turned his pillow over, but was still too hot and troubled to sleep. He wanted out, but his side wouldn't let him go.

"You're a big investment, McShane," he was told. "We need more from you yet. Sure, you know *that* McShane, don't you? For sure, you do."

"Don't you think I've done enough killing, for God's sake?"

"This is war, McShane. You're a combatant and you've got a cause. You're lucky, McShane. What the hell have the British Army got to fight for? Anyway, you can't retire from a war. There's no retirement from war. That's desertion, McShane. Don't go there, son. Anyway, what are you going to do after this? Become a bus driver? I don't think they're looking to recruit the likes of you, son. You're involved in an armed struggle, McShane, and the only way out's in a box. You're fucking lucky. You're trained. You've got expertise. You're lucky you're not one of the ground troops. You're lucky you volunteered for special services– "

"*Was* volunteered."

"Volunteered, and were given what you wanted."

"Bloody hell, Gerrard! This is bloody Belfast, not the siege of Stalingrad."

"Precisely. This is Belfast. And don't go getting yourself captured by the Brits, McShane. We'll know if you surrender. We'll know if you're colluding. And if you do get caught we'll put you on hunger strike before your feet hit a cell floor. Anyway, *faugh a ballagh... tiocfaidh ár la.*"

McShane hated when Gerrard Boyce broke into Irish. McShane was fond of the sound of the mother tongue, but when Boyce spoke it he did so with a machine gun rattle that was almost unintelligible; the words spat out like venom. McShane didn't like it much when Boyce spoke in English either, but could at least interpret the bigoted gibberish.

To speak Irish seemed to be a prerequisite for the serious republican, and McShane's inability to speak it set him apart and was a setback. But McShane didn't care about setbacks; no longer cared about making progress in the organisation. Of late he'd stopped going to the political meetings and regurgitating the Marxist/Leninist ideology and long-winded justifications for the armed struggle. That all seemed immaterial in light of the civilian body count. Nothing could justify that, he believed now. Twenty years of war was a strict test of anybody's propaganda and its influence on him had worn thin. But that was where his thinking stopped; being a contributor to the carnage himself. To think too much was dangerous. In that way lay madness. Madness born of madness.

The killing had been easier when he had had some faith. It had been easier to support the cause as a romantic fifteen-year-old. Then he had believed in a united Ireland without question, and had hurled the bricks and petrol bombs at the Brits with the enthusiasm of a young man fighting for his country. With maturity came disillusionment – a questioning of the motives of his comrades. First he doubted the politics of the struggle, now he doubted the morality of their methods. Suddenly it had all seemed pointless and lacking in reason.

"You can't eat a flag, son," a Derry man had once told him. It rang true.

McShane kicked back the duvet, got up, stretched and hobbled over to the window. The bloody faces were gone now that the dawn light had come. He scanned the parked cars along the terraced street below, looking up towards the Europa and reading each number plate in turn, nearest to furthest, to test his eyesight. Satisfied, McShane shuffled backwards to the bed and sat down to rub his eye to get rid of the soreness from the stick-in-the-eye.

McShane's vision had always been remarkable, even at an early age. That and a slow heart rate had set him apart from the others and recommended him to be trained up for 'sniping'. Though he was physically suitable he was, unknown to his minders, handicapped by a conscience.

Deep in thought, he went to open the bedroom window. His heart sank when he saw Gerrard Boyce's Granada parked across the road. The engine was running. Boyce honked the horn and leaned out of the driver's window the moment he spotted McShane. He gestured for him to come down.

Not an assignment. Oh, God! Please, not an assignment!

McShane hadn't seen Boyce in over a month. Not since the last job; but Boyce, he knew against hope, was due. McShane had been half expecting a visit. But shit! an assignment. Maybe the victim would get a glimpse of him and run off today. Maybe the gun would jam. Maybe he'd be the one to get shot. Maybe he would be blown away by the Brits in an ambush.

McShane was kidding himself – knew he'd get the job done. He always did; always would; was trapped by a bloodlust whose appetite was unrelenting – like the craving of a vampire. His conscience was too fragile – a fine membrane that hadn't quite thickened enough to resist the needle thrusts of the addiction. The repetitious nature of his work had created an easy routine that had hardened him to what he was about to do and had led him towards psychopathy.

McShane threw on jeans, T-shirt and trainers. He'd be getting changed when they got to that day's safe house. Boyce would have clothes in the car with him. New stuff, knocked-off from some large store or factory shop and with the labels cut out. He'd shower then and get a shave. It was the start of a new trail calculated to lead well away from his home where there were so many clues for Special Branch to piece together.

Before leaving he tapped on the door to the spare room. No answer; he opened the door with care. Six o'clock and his wife slept soundly.

"See you later," he mumbled. No answer.

He crept out of the house and over to Boyce's car.

Creeping had become a habit. It was often a necessity. It had given his spine a supine curve reminiscent of a big cat coiled and ready to pounce; the deportment of a predator.

"You took your time, son."

McShane ignored Boyce's bad humour, a device he deduced that Boyce used to assert his rank.

"Where to today?"

"You'll know soon enough. Get in."

Boyce sped off heading north along the Westlink. Before long he pulled into the car park of a shopping centre at the top of the Shore Road. It was busy enough for them to do a rudimentary briefing without drawing attention to themselves.

Boyce handed McShane the customary A4 envelope.

"What the hell's this?" McShane whinged as he pulled out a wodge of photos. There was usually only one. He didn't stop to count the faces.

"Congratulations. Today's going to be spectacular, McShane. Oh, by the way, this is Michael. He'll be working with you."

The rear door on the driver's side opened and a wiry-looking teenager in a Manchester United top slid onto the back seat; he was remarkable only for his slender build and the acne polka-dotting his face. He wasn't much more than a child.

Boyce drove off heading through the streets of Tigers Bay – enemy territory. Soon they were heading up the Antrim Road and turning into the car park of Belfast Zoo. It was a bright spring day and the view across Belfast Lough towards Scotland was stunning.

Moments later a van pulled up alongside. The driver, a short stocky man, produced a couple of hessian sacks from the back, put them in the boot of Boyce's Granada and took off.

"Munitions?"

"Munitions, McShane."

"Mine?"

"Not this time."

"Fuck, Boyce. What are you playing at?"

"It's a new toy for you, son."

"What is it?"

"An AK."

"What do I want with a bloody AK-47, Boyce?"

"Believe me, son, where you're going you're going to need it."

"Look, I'm a specialist, Boyce. You know that! I deal with people one at a time."

"Not today, McShane. Today we're talking volume."

"Come on! That's outrageous!"

"I'd say atrocious. I think we're going to make the front pages tomorrow."

"You're a bloody psycho, Boyce."

"*You're* calling *me* a psycho, McShane? Now that's funny."

"Look, you know I don't do this type of work. You know that damn rightly."

"You are today, son."

"But– "

"Just shut up and listen!"

"But..."

Boyce swung a fist at McShane's face and caught him across his bad eye. Agony.

"Fuck! There's no need for– "

Boyce swung another punch. This time it caught McShane across his right ear. A stinging blow that caused maximum pain.

God! Boyce's good, McShane thought.

"As I say, just shut the fuck up, McShane and listen. Now, your lack of interest in the cause... it's been noticed. Today will be a little reminder of the horror of war for you. A wake-up call. Something to remember the next time you're out there in the field and think twice about what you're doing. It'll remind you of your responsibilities – where your loyalties lie. You see, McShane, I know you. You think you are a virtuoso, a concert pianist. Well, you're not. You're playing a drum in a fucking military band and there's a set rhythm to follow and it's a very simple rhythm... bang, bang, bloody bang, bang. Have you got that McShane? Do I make myself clear?"

McShane said nothing. Another slap caught him on the lip.

"You are not a soloist, McShane. Got it?"

"Yeah," McShane grunted; anything to stop Boyce's slaps and punches. He wondered if the brutality was a show of strength to impress the youngster sitting mute in the back; a frightener to set him off in the right direction along their terrible path. McShane felt sorry for the kid.

Drops of blood started to drip McShane's forensics across the photographs still nestling in his lap. Both men in the front of the car noticed and felt uncomfortable about the careless lapse.

"See this place?" Boyce asked, grabbing the black and white photo sitting on top of the pile and waving it in McShane's face. "A bookies'. Antrim Road, right?"

"Right."

"See them?" Boyce continued, grabbing the next photo.

"Yeah."

"Squaddies."

"Yeah."

"There's four that visit the bookies' on a regular basis. Sometimes there's a fifth, but usually it's just the same four."

"Right."

More blood dripped across the next photo.

"Of course these *eejits* shouldn't be going to a bookies', and especially not on the Antrim Road. It's a breach of their rules. They're straying a bit too far. This one was taken last Friday... this one, the Friday before... and this one, the Friday before that. Every Friday and always at least four of them, see? Here... the fifth one was in last Friday; the chances are he'll be in there today. They're getting lazy, McShane. The same place, at the same time and always the same faces. They must be bloody mad if they think we're not watching them. It'll be like taking candy from a baby!"

"Sick."

"Shut it, McShane!"

This time it was the teenager intervening.

"Who the hell asked you, you pillock?" McShane snapped.

Boyce slapped McShane again. More blood. More evidence, but this time in a fine spray across Boyce's dashboard. Boyce cringed at the mess being made along his mahogany veneer.

"The kid's right. Shut it, McShane. Look... here's the score. I want you two in and out in under a minute, right? Any longer and your driver won't be there to escort you home. Got it?"

McShane nodded.

"If the kid screws up, I'm not hanging around waiting for him. He's on his own, right?" McShane said, turning to look Boyce in the eye.

"Look, Michael here can look after himself. You're the one we're worried about, McShane. You cock this up and you're dead meat."

"Where's the driver?"

"We're getting him now. He's at the safe house."

Half an hour later and they were back in West Belfast. A change of clothes, a wash and shave and McShane felt almost human again – except for the dull throb in his ear and the sharp stinging pain in his eye.

McShane joined the other three men in the backyard of the two-up two-down. The men didn't look up or speak to him. He could sense that there hadn't been much conversation. The butts on the ground told of serious chain-smoking – as if they'd been trying to avoid the job by smoking themselves to death whilst there was still time.

Boyce waved a finger. The driver got up and left without speaking. McShane looked over to Michael and shrugged.

Michael looked away. Within minutes a car drew up and was idling behind the backyard wall. The driver's head appeared round the yard door.

"Ok?"

McShane and Michael lifted their hessian sacks and followed the driver to the car, a Ford Fiesta – nondescript and freshly 'requisitioned' for the cause from round the corner.

Inside the bookies' on the Antrim Road, the commentary from the two o'clock at Chepstow boomed about the room, Peter O'Sullivan chanting the action at a hundred miles an hour as though he were riding among the jockeys.

The room, otherwise, was silent, smoky and half-full. A lazy Friday afternoon ambience permeated wall-to-wall across the lino. No one spoke and no one was bothered when McShane and the boy entered with their sacks.

The two paused in the doorway, dark figures to those inside, their faces hard to see through the cigarette haze and with the sunlight streaming in behind them. Some of the punters looked up and smiled. But then the kid produced his AK and started blasting.

McShane was stunned and closed his eyes – he couldn't bear the look on the kid's face. It was an excited grimace, both concentrated and determined. Pure hate.

An image of his wife came to him. She was at the altar as she had been on their wedding day, smiling and beckoning him: "*I love you Tommy, I love you...*" She looked beautiful, irresistible and in that moment he knew that he loved her too.

As he opened his eyes again to the unfolding carnage, it suddenly struck him: the squaddies weren't there. *They're not bloody here! They're not in the fucking room! None of them!*

But the kid went on firing as blood flew in a shower of red.

4

Crows were pecking on the tin roof of Peggy Smyth's cottage with the rhythm of rain dropping from a tree. At twilight they would head for home, flying down the lough like rags flapping in the wind; black confetti forming a dark mosaic.

The tin had been a temporary measure fifteen years ago, when the thatch was due for renewal. Peggy never found the money for the renovation however, the idea rusting in the memory like the corrugated sheets, now a reddish brown – the colour of tomato soup – and pockmarked with moss; a provider of fast food for the crows on their way back to the rookery.

The cottage, as a thatched cottage, had been picture-postcard perfect, but left much to the imagination now. Hot in summer, cold in winter, the roof accentuated the weather with the efficacy of either an oven or a fridge.

Peggy Smyth had grown deaf to the tapping overhead. The soundtrack that drew her attention was provided by the radio. 'Three' and 'Four' were her choice – a luxury that offered a glimpse of another, more refined world; a departure from the everyday wrestle with the overdraft and the threat of tomorrow's bills.

She couldn't help but notice rain though; a storm could be quite alarming. A heavy downpour excited her; there was something in the thundering rhythm that fired her imagination. It reminded her of her honeymoon in Paris and the first night, sitting on the Rue Des Beaux Arts in St Germain – a humid evening relieved by a cloudburst; she and Owen sheltering under an awning at a roadside *bar tabac*. The raindrops slapped into the pavement with a force that bounced them back into the air in crowns. The two of them watched the torrent from the security of their canopy, huddled together, hands clasped and eyes transfixed, as an old man stares into the embers of a fire.

She had loved Owen. A gentle man. It broke her when he died – the symptoms developing slowly, but then the end coming quick. Myeloma. Cruel on top of her other losses. She never forgave God. Had to blame someone. Then her brother moved in. Poor Ignatius was often punished for not being Owen.

She hated being a widow. Widows were old, wrinkled Greek women veiled head to foot in black cotton. Widows had grey hair, drooping breasts and moustaches; were always glum and moaning, wrapped up in dark shrouds of self-pity and mourning. And Peggy Smyth was too young. She didn't want to become a dried-up prune whilst there was still ripeness in her flesh. Standing naked in front of the mirror at night, she would pat her thighs and bottom checking for excess wobble; would lift a breast to check the sag. And yet there was still a firmness, a voluptuousness going to waste – wasted on the dull routine of her days, weeks and months. And the frustration ate away at her, a growing frustration that nagged at her and made her nag at her brother.

That, she believed, was the glumness of widows: the frustration of being alive, but living half a life. She dreamt of a white knight, but he was a vague and distant figure. A face without features.

"She's going in on Friday, Ignatius. They're doing it then and there. The doctor says if she doesn't have it treated now, it will only cause her problems later. Something about the joint swelling under constant pressure. They've told her it's something to do with alignment. I told her it's something to do with all the carry-outs and junk food she eats. It's a wonder she's never thought of moving to Peking or Delhi. It would save her a small fortune. She's not looking forward to the treatment one bit. I said I hope they know what they're doing and hope they have a sharp knife. She didn't laugh. Says if it all goes wrong I can have her Lladro. I said I'd take it straight down to Cash Converters and have myself a weekend somewhere hot. She said she's going to make sure that she survives the operation rather than see her Lladro given away. Have you ever been into Cash Converters, Iggy? It's brilliant for tellies and hi-fis, for anything really."

Peggy wandered into the lounge, drying a dessert bowl. She was checking whether, though silent, her brother had been listening to any of the news she had harvested for him at the checkout in the local 'Co'; she'd know by his expression.

She was aware, however, of an ominous silence in the front lounge only contradicted by the telly squawking in the corner; a familiar sound she hated. He was watching an episode of *One Foot in the Grave.* How appropriate, she thought. The television had become an insurmountable barrier to conversation between brother and sister.

Peggy had never been close to her brother Iggy. But that they were brother and sister, they had little in common. They wouldn't have been friends. They were very different in personality – few would have guessed that they were even related. Peggy, brash and outgoing, would speak her mind; Ignatius, more ponderous and self-absorbed, was introverted and shy. They had also inherited physical characteristics from different branches of the family tree. Whilst Peggy was tall, blonde and curvy, Ignatius was short, dark and thin-boned.

"You should have been a Small, not a Smyth. Smyths aren't small, Smyth," their late father used to chant at the boy.

"Are you listening to me? For God's sake, Ignatius, it's like living in a silent order – the Nistercians or something."

"Cistercians."

"Nistercians, Cistercians... neither of them have got much to say for themselves."

Peggy stood over her brother rubbing the bowl with a tea cloth as if to summon a genie.

Ignatius Smyth ignored his sister, his eyes transfixed by the images flickering before him on the screen. It was the nine o'clock news. Peggy didn't see the lead item or hear the commentary, "...*eight people were killed in the betting office shooting. Three more were admitted to hospital with gunshot wounds – two are thought to be in a critical condition.*

A spokesman for the RUC told reporters at the scene that nothing could justify an act of this kind:

'I would appeal to both sides of the community to stay calm and would like to reassure all parties that the security forces are applying every resource to apprehending whoever is responsible for this shooting. We will not rest until we bring a successful conclusion to our enquiries. We urge members of the public to help us find the perpetrators of this crime and will treat any information received in the strictest confidence.'"

Peggy wandered back to the kitchen to put away the dried bowl and pick up another wet one.

"Did you hear anything I said about Mrs Logan, Iggy? She gets her operation on Friday. Local anaesthetic. She's really put out. Doesn't know if she can face it. I hope she's doing the right thing, Iggy... Iggy? Ignatius! For God's sake, Iggy, I might as well talk to my bucking self!" Peggy moaned, as she clomped back into the lounge.

But he was gone, the seat empty save for the impression left by his backside in the Dralon, a hollow accentuated by years of sitting in front of the television. A heavy investment. Peggy hadn't heard the door slam. He must have closed it so as not to disturb her. Perhaps he thought she might try and stop him from leaving. He didn't want to have to explain where he was going and why, if she did.

Peggy glanced at the TV. Trouble in Belfast. She walked over and switched it off. Too familiar – too depressing.

5

"The dogs in the street know it's Marty McGowan. McGowan, McGowan, McGowan. It's the one name that comes up every time."

It was mid-morning and copy deadlines were pressing in the editorial offices of the *Telegraph*. A fraught half hour and Dillon Jenkins was struggling to get his message across to his editor. It was an important message – an exposé. McGowan, according to Jenkins' source, was *the* key player in expanding the drugs market in North Belfast. Jenkins believed he had the scoop, but his editor couldn't or wouldn't see it that way.

"How do you spell 'accommodate', Dillon? For God's sake, you can't even spell, man! There's two 'c's and two bloody 'm's. How can you expect anyone to read this crap if you can't even spell it?"

Jenkins ducked in time to avoid the ball of paper coming straight at his head.

"God, Dillon! I'm going to have to move you onto the effing crossword page if you don't start delivering. Or how are you at writing horoscopes?"

Dillon Jenkins' editor was no renaissance man. He was barely a 'man' at all – more a cartoon character. Elmer Fudd maybe, or Clark Kent's editor in the *Superman* strip. And Jenkins couldn't look him in the eye. He knew if he did, his attention would be drawn to the man's reddening cheeks and the balls of sweat running across his brow. The sight would bring on an expression of revulsion that the editor could instantly read in Dillon's eyes and just make him madder. And then the vein that curled a crooked path across the editor's temple down towards his right ear would start throbbing. Jenkins would then grimace and have to look away again.

He was staring down onto what was left of the carpet. An historical relic. A skeleton of a thousand threads. It reminded him of the headmaster's office at school.

"Look, I'm sorry. You've got to under– "

"And there's a bloody split infinitive in the third sentence. And the third. Hang on... and the fifth. Oh! And the second paragraph is ten lines long and comprises one sentence with absolutely no effing punctuation whatsoever – not even a bloody comma, Dillon!"

Ted Montgomery's wit was merciless.

"Ted, it's– "

"It's effing useless, that's what it is. And don't dare argue with me, Dillon. I know my English."

"No, you're right, Ted. I can't."

Jenkins knew what was coming next.

"For someone who's worked in Fleet Street, Dillon, some of your work's pretty sloppy."

That stung. But Jenkins expected it. It was Montgomery's most lethal weapon, they both knew, and he used it often.

Jenkins suspected that Montgomery would never forgive him for his Fleet Street experience. That his recent job history was well documented and known to the *Tele*'s management, was a smoking gun that could be used against him any time. Jenkins' agenda was obvious to everyone and was one that made him unpopular on the Belfast paper. It was a familiar story: Fleet Street reporter makes a name for himself, takes to the drink, cocks up, rehabilitates, takes to drink again, cocks up, is demoted, drops out, dries out, takes off to the provinces to start afresh.

So here he was. Problem: a recognised name in the trade; over-qualified for his new position; struggling; resented; unloved; not easy.

"No, you're right. I'll go over it. It'll be fine once I've finished, Ted. Don't worry; I'll knock it into shape. It'll be fine."

"No, the bloody subs will, Dillon. That's what they're paid for. It's more just the principle."

"No. I'll have another go."

Jenkins bent down and retrieved the curled-up hard copy proof he had submitted to Montgomery earlier. He knew it would be better to make a tactical retreat than to stand his ground. He would get home the sooner for it. He returned to his desk and computer terminal without further confrontation. Montgomery felt he had made his point – his door slammed to indicate the end of the matter, punctuating the conversation with a perfectly timed full stop.

Jenkins worked on through the afternoon and into the early evening by which time the office, in a dull grey light, resembled a cell. The ticking of a wall clock brought some relief; a reminder that there could come an end to the working day. But the hunched silhouettes of the subs on the late shift told of hours unwinding in slow motion.

Jenkins was fighting off lethargy. He had to finish the piece for the Thursday editions, but as things were, it looked as if it wouldn't squeeze its way into the paper until the weekend now, if at all. Dedication had already prolonged his captivity well beyond the departure of the nine-to-fivers. He had smoked on through the evening and into the night, struggling to tease the appropriate words onto the screen before tiredness tied his brain in knots.

There were few words to describe drug trafficking in Northern Ireland that hadn't been used before. The mainstream politicians had nothing new to say. The RUC press office had supplied the same gloomy statistics. The paramilitaries had issued their usual denials.

The emergence of the drugs market was a story that needed to be told, but was one that no one wanted to hear. Not now.

Not in Belfast where people were preoccupied with avoiding bombs and bullets. And not in Westminster, where the Government was preoccupied with breaking the unions and pushing through the Poll Tax.

By four in the morning however, Jenkins had found an angle he reckoned he could flesh out and that his editor would print. It excluded McGowan.

A pity. McGowan was the main man, *the* leading character in the story: a drugs overlord, a paramilitary, a thug, a Belfast warlord with a large investment in other people's misery. And he was untouchable. He had friends in the very highest places, which gave him political muscle – and in the lowest, providing the brawn to flex it. He was well protected. There was a time when Jenkins would have had no fear in naming McGowan, but Jenkins was clawing his way up the greasiest of poles from the bottom. He was in no position to make autocratic decisions. McGowan's was a name Jenkins would not be using in print. Not yet. Not without Montgomery's say-so. It would have to wait. His investigative piece was dressed in more general tones and subtle hints. It would keep the story alive a little longer. He hoped it would satisfy his sources and wouldn't make him a target.

The later the hour, the harder to leave. No matter how much he wanted to be home it was easier to find some minor task to keep him at work. The cage door was open, but he couldn't seize the opportunity of escape. When he found himself dozing over the keyboard however, he decided he'd had enough. He transferred his copy over to the subs desk, switched off his computer and grabbed his coat.

"Got any change?" a voice croaked from inside a pile of cardboard boxes out on the street.

"Sorry mate," Jenkins lied. He hated lies.

He crossed the road bemused. Tramps were a rarity in Belfast. That part of Belfast. Outside the *Tele* in particular.

It was dry on the street. A relief. Rain had marred much of April. Maybe May would be better. Dawn was coming; a slither of salmon pink across an azure sky. Jenkins squeezed in behind the steering wheel and shoved in a cassette.

He caught a glimpse of himself in the driver's mirror. His eyes were bloodshot from staring into the computer screen all day and his hair desperate: thick, dark, curly and overgrown. If he looked this knackered at thirty-four, he wondered how he would look at forty.

He pulled away from his car parking space and headed for home with the Chet Baker Quartet for company – as cool and soothing as vanilla ice cream – and unaware of the character in the olive parka in the doorway of the Poundstretcher across the road, committing Jenkins' registration number to memory.

Mist hung at head height on the Ballyblessington ring road. The dual carriageway bypassed the urban sprawl of Ballyblessington New Town on the drive from Belfast along the Ards Peninsula. By day it was a busy commuter link, but now lay deserted. Clean and black, it looked new in the dawn light – almost photogenic.

As Jenkins approached the last section of ring road before his turn-off he wound down the window a slither, which gave vent to a cloud of cigarette smoke before the dewy morning air seeped in.

Jenkins took the roundabout as if steering a Scalextric car – gentle hands, tempo steady.

As he crossed the junction to take the back road to the seaside town of Fellrock, a pile of something caught his eye on the traffic island. Some rags? A body, maybe.

Jenkins brought the car to a halt alongside the island. Engine idling, the tape machine clicked off interrupting Chet Baker in full flow. Jenkins nudged the driver's door with his shoulder. The door popped open as if caught by a gust of wind and then stopped abruptly when its bottom lip bit into the pavement with a crunch. The force shook some dust off the door panel, revealing that the grey car, a battered Zodiac, could be cream when washed.

Another cloud of cigarette smoke billowed through the doorway and clung about Jenkins like ectoplasm as he emerged onto the road: a massive bulk, baggy-clothed and tottering. It took a huge effort to stand upright and then reach the pavement. Stretching, he staggered a step or two before pausing and yawning as if to swallow the sky. Then a lollop across the short distance to the island, where he could now see that the mystery bundle was a man, slumped – half sitting, half lying – against the white bollard, centre stage.

"Oh, God! It's you, Smyth," he said, recognising the guy from the local tyre shop. "What the hell are you doing here?"

No answer. Jenkins' Home Counties accent had a volume and enthusiasm that easily irritated.

"Hey, seriously. Are you ok? Can I give you a lift?" Jenkins continued, bending down to get a closer look.

Still no answer.

"Can I give you a lift?" Jenkins asked again, raising his voice as though Smyth might be deaf.

"Nagh," Smyth grunted after a long pause.

"What's up? Are we feeling the worse for wear?"

"Nagh."

"What's wrong then?"

"Arseholes like you."

"Wha– "

"Arseholes like you keep pestering me."

"Ah."

Jenkins sat down and leaned against the bollard beside Smyth. He assumed Smyth's slump and lit a fag.

"I hope you're not thinking of staying, Englishman."

"Fag?" Jenkins asked, rattling the packet towards Smyth's face.

"No. No thanks."

"Well, Smyth– "

"Look, why don't you piss off and give my head peace, you English twat?"

"I'm not."

"Not what?"

"English. I'm Welsh."

"Well, you don't bloody sound it."

"Oh, the accent? My dad moved to London before I was born. He's from near Cardiff originally; from Barry. It's the Blackpool of Wales. My grandfather had an ice cream parlour on Barry Island. He invented an ice cream called the– "

"You sound bloody English to me."

"Called the *North Pole*... My name's Dillon, Dillon Jenkins. Doesn't sound very English, does it?"

"No, just fecking awful. Anyway, I can smell the blood of an Englishman a mile off and you smell like one to me."

"Thanks a bunch," Jenkins said, flicking his unfinished cigarette halfway across the street.

"Fee-fi-fo-fum, I smell the blood of an Englishman!" Smyth sang in a slow and scary voice. It spooked Jenkins.

"Fee-fi-fo– "

"Right. I'm off. Do you want a lift or not, Smyth?"

"No."

"Oh, come on. It's too far to walk."

"Look *Dillon*, I'm not going anywhere. I can't move."

Jenkins had never heard his name sound so ugly.

"Look, what's the matter, Smyth? You haven't broken a leg or anything have you?"

"Do I really look like I've broken something? Don't you think I'd at least be moaning a bit if I had?"

"So why can't you move?"

"None of your business."

"Right. This is your last chance," Jenkins said, rolling onto his feet and prising himself off the ground with two hands whilst using the bollard as a lever.

Silence.

"'Bye, then."

Jenkins hobbled back to the car, whose engine was still idling at the kerbside.

"Bye, *Englishman*," Smyth snarled, making the words sound like an accusation.

Jenkins yanked the driver's door shut behind him, gritting his teeth as the bottom edge scraped back across the kerb. He rested his forehead on the steering wheel to refocus and then with a loud *"Fuck it!"* turned the engine off, fought his way out of the car and waddled back over to the island.

"How long have you been sitting here, Smyth?" Jenkins asked, crouching down on his haunches.

"What's it to you?"

"Oh, come on. How long?"

"Since midnight."

"Ok. So why? You can't be very comfortable."

"What's it to you?"

"Oh, for God's sake! Please, just tell me," Jenkins pleaded, clasping his hands to his face in frustration.

"I'll tell you what. I'll tell you what I'm doing here if you promise to piss off and leave me alone."

"Ok."

Silence.

"Oh, come on, tell me!"

"Well, I'm sitting down."

"Yes, I can see that, you muppet. And?"

"Look, you wouldn't understand. Anyway I'm not bloody telling you now. Not if you're going to take the piss."

"Oh, for Pete's sake, just tell me and I'll go away!"

"No, no. I can't. I'd feel stupid."

"Well, you kind of look stupid, anyway– "

"IT'S A FUCKING SIT-DOWN PROTEST. ALL RIGHT?"

"Ok, ok. No need to shout. Mmm, a sit-down protest? Really? I thought they went out of fashion in the sixties."

"Oh, piss off."

"So what brought this on, Smyth? Bored with life in suburbia?"

"I thought you were going to– "

"Well, let's face it, you don't strike me as being one of the world's great political thinkers."

"Look. I'm being serious here. It was the shooting– "

"The shooting?"

"The bookies'."

"Eight dead? The Antrim Road?"

Smyth nodded.

"Does my head in."

"Nasty. But aren't you used to all that stuff by now, Smyth?"

"Don't be ridiculous."

Jenkins paused. Lit another cigarette.

"Anyway, I'd have thought that if you're going to make a political gesture– "

"This isn't political."

"Well, if you *were* going to make a political gesture, I'd have thought you could find a better place than this to stage it."

"What the hell would you know?"

"I'm a journalist."

"Well, I don't need the likes of you here– "

"Oh, come on. We're not all doorsteppers, three-in-a-bed-sex-romp-exposé writers. Some of us serve quite a mundane function."

"Like leeches – to help us bleed."

"Look, I'm just a guy on his way home from work. Right now I've had journalism up to here. Anyway, as I was saying, if you want to make a political gesture (and anyway, all protests are political), you've got to do it where you can be seen and heard. Somewhere where people will take notice of you. Somewhere like the City Hall or Stormont. Not on an insignificant traffic island and definitely not at four in the morning when everyone else is asleep. And another thing – you need a few more people, preferably a hundred or a thousand. And you need them sitting on the road, or lying across it. You know, a major obstruction. Stop the traffic. To anybody passing by right now, you look like a drunk, or the victim of a violent crime – not the *generalissimo* of a major political campaign."

"I told you. This isn't political. And it's not a campaign. It's a bloody protest, ok?"

"All right, so what's your wife going to say, when she notices that you haven't come home?"

"What would you know about that?"

"And you'll be due in at work in about five hours' time, I presume."

"Look man, not that it's any of your business, but I'm not going back to work."

"Oh."

"And don't patronise me, ok? If you don't like what I'm doing then go away. This is a personal protest and I'm not budging until the killing stops. It's that simple."

"Smyth, if you want to sit here all day then go right ahead. But thank God summer's coming, that's all I'll say. Look, are you absolutely sure I can't give you a lift?"

Smyth shook his head.

"Right. 'Bye then. Oh, and by the way... did you phone the press? Have you informed the media – the RUC?"

"Oh, bugger off and leave me alone. For God's sake... *please, just go!*"

Jenkins pushed himself upright and walked back to the Zodiac. After a bit of clunking and scraping, the engine started and the car crawled away leaving a slim, vapour-like trail of fumes.

Before the Zodiac had travelled the length of a football pitch however, it braked and idled for a few seconds before reversing to its original spot, making a high-pitched whine. More clunking and scraping, followed by the reappearance of Dillon Jenkins' ample silhouette. Jenkins ambled round to the boot from which he produced a brown paper bag. Having checked the contents, he tucked the package under his arm and sauntered over to Smyth, still slumped against the bollard.

"I'm sorry Smyth, but you really are starting to interest me."

Smyth sighed with renewed agitation.

"What?" he asked, turning to look into Jenkins' eyes.

"This isn't Mississippi, you know."

"*What?*"

"This isn't Mississippi," Jenkins said, then paused for further effect. "It might be pleasant hanging out on the streets on a warmer than average night in April, but what happens in January when the temperature's minus two? Not particularly conducive to sitting out all night protesting, then."

"What are you on, Englishman?"

"All I'm saying, Smyth, is that you haven't planned this sit-in... demo... or whatever it is, very carefully, have you? You haven't told the press. You haven't told the police. I bet you haven't even told your family– "

"So bloody what?"

"And you've picked the wrong place – you should be in the city centre. You've picked the wrong country – your balls are going to freeze off in the winter, and– "

"Look, if you don't like the weather here in Northern Ireland– "

"I don't think you understand what I'm trying to say, Smyth. But I bet you won't be here come tomorrow night. Probably this afternoon. Actually, I'll give you until breakfast."

"If this wasn't a sit-down protest for peace, I'd stand up and knock your block off!"

"That's more like it. Fighting talk. That'll help you through those cold winter nights. For that I'll give your protest until tomorrow lunchtime; maybe the afternoon. But look, if you're going to make this work, you've got to have a plan... a strategy. You're going to have to find out how to use the system. You're going to have to put your case on radio. Get on TV. Give interviews. Get your voice heard. Debate, observe and articulate."

"You're wrong, Englishman."

"Why?"

"I've got something much more powerful than talk."

"What's that, then?"

"Passion."

Jenkins sat down and lit another cigarette.

"Well, I've got something stronger than passion."

"What?"

"Spirit."

"Spirit?"

"Yeah, spirit. 14 per cent proof. Black Bush. One bottle of. And by the way..."

"What?" Smyth asked, reaching out to take the bottle from Jenkins, who had produced it from the paper bag like a magician.

"I'm not English."

Smyth took two or three long gulps of whiskey, then wiped his mouth on his sleeve with the graceful swish of a violinist's bow.

"You still sound like one to me, Dillon. Anyway, *Iechyd da!*"

"Slainte!"

6

Hugh Campbell kicked out at the lawnmower – his left foot connecting with the front mudguard producing a loud clang; the metal toecap of his boot proving an excellent clapper. The force of the strike threw him backwards, however. Toppling and over-balanced, he staggered into a tumble that landed him on his bottom, and then into a roll until he came to rest flat on his back in the middle of the field; a position which provided a sweeping view of the spring sky – blue and untainted by cloud.

Campbell took a deep breath. His toe was sore now. He flopped over, wrestled himself back up, brushed the grass cuttings out of his hair, retrieved his hat – brown shapeless felt – and wiped his brow. He stamped his foot in frustration. It was hot for the time of year – hot for Northern Ireland at any time of year; maybe low twenties. Even with heat haze, the view across Strangford Lough was eye-catching, but he had no time for it now. He needed to get the lawn cut (about an acre of the stuff) and fast, since he was needed at his next job by one.

Campbell had to cut a lot of grass to make a living. He usually insisted on using his own mower as part of his gardening service, but Mr McGowan – this morning's client – had requested the use of *his* machine, and McGowan was not a man to be argued with. Campbell, McGowan had instructed, was to use the sit-on that had just been delivered from a dealership in Galway. It was large and fancy and brand new: "The best that money can buy. The mother of all mowers. Like a Ferrari, real quality, but a wee bit slower," McGowan had boasted. Fine. But it had come without operating instructions and no one could fathom how it worked or what it could do. Even starting it was a problem.

Campbell would have refused to do the job, but he wouldn't, or couldn't refuse Mr McGowan. No one refused McGowan.

But Campbell cursed himself for giving in. Why had he agreed to use McGowan's damn mower? He should have employed subterfuge, found a pretext, an excuse to delay the launch of the big red one the moment it was put to him. McGowan knew little of gardening and nothing at all of gardening machinery.

"*Oh, the blades need bedding in, sir. You can't mow with the blades set like that, Mr McGowan. The grass will take months to recover,*" Campbell should have said, or some such other nonsense. But he had just grunted in submission.

Campbell's lack of mental agility had him stuck and struggling with the bloody thing now. He was short of time and panicking. He cursed himself because he knew that he wouldn't have got into this kind of mess if he hadn't accepted the three grand loan that McGowan had forced on him in the middle of the winter. Campbell had been desperate to keep his gardening business ticking over through a lean spell – the weather had been severe, work had been slack and it looked as if Campbell and Sons might go under. McGowan had been generous, but both men knew there would be a price.

Campbell tried the ignition key again. *Agh! Thank the Lord!* This time she started. *Must have been flooded,* he thought, looking up towards the house for a reaction.

McGowan was standing in the conservatory window leaning on the shoulder of his right-hand man, Lexy Danvers, a thug – thick-set, stocky and shaven-headed – whom Campbell thought hung around McGowan like an organ grinder's monkey. McGowan gave Campbell a nod, then raised his glass. Campbell returned a forced smile, almost a grimace, and prepared to drive off, wiping sweat from his brow and thinking, *The man's got more money than sense.*

That McGowan had disposable income, a large disposable income, was apparent from the material wealth on show around his estate – from the ostentatious BMW, to the new-build house with indoor pool and jacuzzi. McGowan clinked with the tinkle of gold jewellery – heavy, gaudy chains that swung about his wrists and neck; a thick neck sitting on an over-pumped chest that undulated like the hills of Down. There had been plenty of time to body-build when McGowan had served time at Her Majesty's pleasure – seven years for armed robbery; out in three and a half. But that was back in the seventies. He was a reformed character now. No more getting his hands dirty. The dirty work was delegated.

Like many in the district, Hugh Campbell had been pleased when the Old Manse was sold. A local landmark property, it had sat on the lough shore at Kilcarron for over a hundred and twenty years. The sale came following a generation of neglect and a final year of decline whilst the house languished on the property market, empty after the death of its elderly owner.

The local community hoped that the Georgian property and gardens would be saved and renovated by the purchaser, who, rumour had it, was a wealthy businessman from Belfast. They imagined that he would prove to be an asset to the village; be a benefactor. None had envisaged that the Manse would be demolished overnight before local opposition could be galvanised. The site was cleared to make room for a new house – fully insulated and featureless – and then, not only cleared of the old house, but also of the old walled garden and within it, the rose garden.

The loss of the rose garden had upset Campbell most. His grandfather had planted it for the original owners before the turn of the century and his father had inherited its care, as had Hugh in his turn. Hugh had continued to tend it for the next thirty years, even until recently when the house had lain vacant and the work had gone unpaid.

Campbell therefore, resented having to work for McGowan,

but couldn't afford to refuse his cash. He was caught in a money trap and hated it.

McGowan gave Campbell another wave before moving back from the conservatory windows and sinking into the depths of an armchair while deep in conversation with his monkey.

The sit-on moved off with a juddering shudder and a grinding of gears as Campbell mistimed the release of the clutch. Man and machine lurched away from the house and across the newly-grown lawn, down over the brow of the hill and on towards the sea, leaving a broad band of lime green stubble in their wake.

"Of course I'm nervous, Lexy. The consignment's worth two million on the street. It's well worth the risk, but it's still a risk. Look, I'm not in the risk business, I'm in the making money business. That's all. But if this bloody journalist, Jenkins, has wind of this, then we could be stuffed. I'm not about to get buggered about because of some hack."

"I can have him silenced today. This morning. Whenever you like."

"Look, let's not be too hasty about this, Lexy. The guy needs handling. You know, steered in the right direction. He doesn't need a spanking. Not yet, anyway."

Marty McGowan took a sip of gin and tonic from the tall glass clasped in the fingers tattooed 'love'. This hand was the wife of the pair – the worker. Productive. The other hand, with the fingers labelled 'hate', was for punching and jabbing – the enforcer. Destructive.

"It's a watch and wait brief, Lexy," he continued. "From what I've heard, he's a bit flaky. A sensitive flower. And if he pokes his nose in too far, it'll just need a sharp slap to set him straight," McGowan added, swinging the hand called 'hate' through the air, shadow-boxing. "He'll be easy."

"We could do more, Marty," Lexy Danvers suggested casually. He was lounging across the large leather sofa opposite

McGowan. Like McGowan he was staring at the old gardener working his way up and down the lawn, watching him disappear then reappear over the brow of the hill down by the lough shore. Danvers should have been comfortable slouched across the cream calf's leather couch, but the conservatory was too hot and he was perspiring profusely in the fierce sunlight. He wouldn't complain however; not if McGowan was happy.

"No, Lexy. N... O... The paper won't let him off the leash on this one, anyway. It's all tittle-tattle and hearsay. What can he know? A name or two? Some local gossip?"

"Well, we're keeping a close eye on him."

"Fine. Look, if he does know more than we think and tries to run with it – you know, the big story – well, there's plenty we can do."

"Why don't we leak him something... a morsel, a harmless titbit... see what he does with it? We might get an inkling of how much he really knows."

"I think he knows bugger all, Lexy, to be honest."

"Exactly. If we feed him a story and he runs with it, it'll prove he's got nothing better to write about and we're in the clear."

"Mmm, a plant. Not bad, Lexy," McGowan mumbled, pausing for thought. "Ok. We'll give it a go. Yeah, let's not hang around. We'll feed him a story this week and see if it runs."

"You know, I think he could be useful to us– "

"Ok. Anyway, I'm sure he'd like to get the hell out of here and back to London. Maybe we can help him on his way. I've heard that if he keeps his nose clean and keeps off the booze for three or four months, he'll be away."

"That's a big 'if'."

"Sure. Well, if he doesn't go, if he becomes a nuisance, we always have a last resort. But let's not go there, Lexy. Journalists don't make good victims. They look after their own. They're almost as bad as the cops on that score. And no one's going to thank us for stirring things up in our own backyard."

McGowan was surprised by Danvers' ingenuity. He wasn't aware that Danvers was capable of original thought. It was unsettling. Danvers wasn't paid to think. Danvers was paid to agree. To agree and enact. McGowan usually considered the creativity of others a threat to his autonomy.

Marty McGowan got up and wandered back over to the conservatory window. He scanned the garden for Campbell, but couldn't see him as he was out of sight of the house on the far side of the hill, down towards the lane running along the lough shore.

Campbell was back off the sit-on and struggling to remove the spark plug. The mower had stalled.

"Where's that *eejit*, Campbell?" McGowan mumbled under his breath, 'hate' twitching with malice. "Anyway, what do you think of the new water feature, Lexy?" he asked, distracted and trying to suppress his impatience.

McGowan was looking across the patio to where two intertwining pelicans had been captured in grey concrete and were spewing a sprinkling of tap water.

"Class, Marty. Real class."

"No, it's shite, Lexy. This is all fucking shite. But do you know why I like it? Because it gets up the noses of my middleclass neighbours. They can't stand it. They can't stand the ostentation. Well, sod them! There's nothing they can do about it."

McGowan rolled 'hate' up into a ball and admired the resultant fist – the fingers taut like the rope in a Turk's head knot. He rubbed it into his other palm, as if shining an apple. Meanwhile, across the lawn, Campbell had taken his leave and slipped away to his one o'clock appointment before finishing the lawn. He would take his chances with McGowan later.

7

Ballyblessington bypass. The sun rises ablaze in yellow. Today will be hot; the streets parched, the air thick and heavy.

By nine o'clock the dual carriageway had lost any semblance of attractiveness. A choking dust was rising from its twin lanes which were now swamped by a flood of traffic becalmed in the rush hour. A stagnant pool. Cars braked and accelerated, jarring tired limbs awake. Breakneck speed and then nothing, no movement, inertia and then whiplash.

Windscreens framed the angst expressions of office workers who, alert to the possibility of delay, stamped on their pedals – desperate to jump another place in the crawl to the city. Adrenaline coursed whilst arms flailed angry hands, tensing into fists or springing into the two-fingered salute.

Vehicles were bottlenecking around the junctions strung along the bypass, their flow restricted to a trickle. Amidst the congestion brakes squeaked and horns honked and time passed in mouse years. From the back of those cars on the school run, bright eyes blinked on the faces of children shocked by the madness of adults and traumatised by the relentless routine. For them, the God of work seemed cruel.

On the Fellrock roundabout a dog barked; its howls audible above the traffic hum. The sandy-coloured mongrel was directing its voice at the two men slumped against the bollard on the island opposite. Despite its bark the dog looked friendly enough – its tail wagging. The men slept. Beside them, a dead bottle of Black Bush. Soon they stirred, woken by the constant din of the traffic and the persistent yapping of the dog, and then leapt to their feet shouting as the dog approached and tried to cock its leg against their bollard.

"Do you think you could do something about that bloody dog, Smyth?" Jenkins moaned, as he fingered the crevasses of his brow to soothe the hangover taking root.

"Do what? And in the meantime I suppose you'd like room service to bring you a nice cup of tea, a pair of slippers and your daily newspaper?"

"Yes, that would be rather nice."

"Go on get! Geet-yah!" Smyth snarled at the dog, which retreated to the roundabout opposite with its tail between its legs. It lay on its stomach watching them in silence from a grassy patch on the far side.

The men sat down.

"It seems you've picked a canine toilet for your protest."

Smyth reacted with an expression that was almost a smile. Taken aback, Jenkins wondered if he had imagined the minuscule movement.

"You're still here, Mr Jenkins. I thought you'd have left hours ago," Smyth said, renewing hostilities.

"Well, I knew you didn't really want me to."

"Oh, is that right?"

"And how's your head, Smyth? Are you ready for the long haul?"

"I'm fine. Well, mostly."

The conversation stalled.

"Smyth?"

"Yes?"

"This isn't a hunger strike is it, by any chance?"

"What?"

"Well, aren't you even a little bit peckish? I know I'm bloody starving. How about a fry? I'd kill for some life-threateningly fatty food."

"Are you trying to tempt me, Englishman?"

"No, no, not at all. I'm just wondering what your plans are

for this morning. You're not really going to sit here all day, are you?"

"You know I am."

"Oh, right. I guess I was just hoping– "

"I'm staying, Mr Jenkins, for however long it takes."

"All right then. But I, for one, have to be going. I've things to do, people to meet, you know. Oh, and what about Mrs Smyth?"

"*Mrs Smyth*? Do you know something, Mr Jenkins?"

"What?"

"You ask too many questions."

"Well, never mind. I'm off now, anyway. Is there anything I can do for you?"

"Yes."

"What?"

"Don't come back."

"Now, you know you don't really mean that. Look, I'll stop by on my way home from work this afternoon. Oh yeah, and I'll bring you some pepper."

"Pepper?"

"Yeah. Dogs hate it."

Jenkins twisted round onto his side and looked over to the quizzical faces staring out of the traffic queue. Grimacing, he levered himself onto his knees and then up onto his feet with the aid of the bollard. It rocked under his weight, nudging Smyth off-balance, who rolled his eyes.

The effort of getting up and walking encouraged Jenkins' hangover to mutate into a thumping headache. His digestive system and kidneys were also complaining by aching in spasms, which in turn brought on waves of nausea. It was a physical state that had become all too familiar. He paused to let the symptoms pass, encouraged with a small belch.

"Good luck, Smyth. I think you'll need it," Jenkins muttered. He turned to walk to his car, still parked at the kerb, whilst shaking his limbs loose to get the blood flowing. About to open the driver's door, he noticed a motorcycle approaching the roundabout at speed. It was white, with a fairing covered in yellow fluorescent flashes – a police bike.

The rider decelerated then pulled up a few yards behind Jenkins' Zodiac, balancing in mid-air for a second before planting a black boot onto the pavement with a crunch. The policeman swung the other leg over the back of the machine in well-practised fashion. A handgun sat proud on the belt straddling the girth of his heavy jacket. The cop rested the machine on its side-stand then produced a clipboard from one of the panniers at the back, ignoring Jenkins, whilst glancing at Smyth.

Looking back towards the bollard, Jenkins noticed that the traffic flow had been slowed still further by those rubbernecking at the unfolding drama.

The policeman raised his visor and stomped over to the bollard as fast as his riding breeches would allow, stopping short of Smyth's feet to tower over him and engulf him in shadow. Smyth's head was barely level with the knees of the policeman, who at first said nothing whilst he scribbled furiously onto his clipboard.

What the hell has he got to write down except the time, date and location? Jenkins wondered, tutting. Meanwhile Smyth sat silent and impassive, trying to ignore the policeman as if he were invisible, which – save for the bare pink hand writing notes and the brown eyes staring expressionless from inside the crash helmet – he was.

When the policeman spoke, Jenkins, who was standing about twenty feet away, had to strain to hear the words; his fingers still gripping the driver's door handle.

"Good morning, sir. We know we can't sit here all day, don't we?" the RUC man said, with the slow drawl of a Wild West sheriff. "And I know you've been here a while. I spotted you and your colleague earlier this morning on my way to work."

The RUC man paused, giving Smyth the chance to offer an

explanation. Experience had taught the officer that those with something to hide are often those with plenty to say – that nervousness loosens the tongue. But Smyth was saying nothing.

"Maybe he's a bit wary of your gun," Jenkins suggested, as he wandered over.

"And whom might we be, sir?"

"Jenkins, Dillon Jenkins. Pleased to make your acquaintance, officer."

Jenkins offered his hand. It was ignored.

"*Dillon?* Like the rabbit in the *The Magic Roundabout*, sir?"

"It's Welsh," Smyth interjected from ground level. "He says he's Welsh, but he doesn't sound very Welsh to me."

"No. That's definitely an English accent, isn't it? Fancy an Englishman impersonating a Welshman. Criminal, I'd say, criminal. Right! I take it you two are an item, then? Ok, which one's Bonnie and which one's Clyde? Or are we Morecambe and Wise today? I see we've been having a bit of a party?"

The policeman prodded his foot at the bottle of Black Bush which was pointing accusingly towards Smyth's midriff.

"Err, that's mine, officer. Sorry, I should have disposed of it earlier," Jenkins said, gingerly.

"Mmm, yes indeed. It's a good job you didn't get into your car and drive off under the influence of this little lot, eh?"

"You don't really think I'd be drinking whiskey this early in the morning, do you officer? It was just a wee dram for him. It's medicinal. He's been sitting out in the cold all night. Anyway, I've got work to do this afternoon. And lots of it."

"Nothing about you would surprise me, sir. But since you seem capable of walking from A to B in a straight line, I'll give you the benefit of the doubt. Anyway, as it happens, I've left my breathalyser back at the station– "

"Oh."

"However, I think it's time you took yourself off now. And please, take this with you," the officer said, dangling the Bush bottle between thumb and forefinger as if it were a used condom. "We don't want to end up getting fined for littering the street now, do we sir?"

"No, no, of course not," Jenkins said with a sheepish grin, as he took the bottle from the policeman's leather-clad hand.

"Off we go then, Mr Jenkins."

The policeman turned to continue his dialogue with Smyth.

"Err, actually, I'm trying to help this man," Jenkins countered, standing his ground.

"No he bloody isn't! Why don't you just shove off and leave me be, Englishman?"

"Good idea. Why don't you?" the policeman said with growing impatience. "You're not making things any easier for this gentleman. He's already guilty of consuming an alcoholic beverage in a public place and, for all I know, he could be drunk and disorderly. He's also loitering with intent and obstructing the Queen's highway. You don't want to be charged with being an accessory, do you?"

"Certainly not, officer."

"Right, enough of the bullshit. This is what we're going to do, gentlemen. You're going to go to work, Mr Jenkins, and you're going to clear off home, Mr... Mr?"

"Smyth."

"Mr Smyth. That's Smyth with a 'y', I take it? Yes, the tyre fitter from Fellrock."

"He's an ex-tyre fitter, now."

"Mmm, home it is then," the officer said, jotting on his pad with gusto.

"I'm afraid I can't move," Smyth said, defiantly.

"Well, if you're injured, Mr Smyth, we'll just have to waste a small fortune in taxpayers' money and order you an ambulance. I'm afraid I can't let you sit here all day. You're a hazard to traffic. You'll cause an accident before long."

"How the hell are *those* cars going to have an accident? I've seen hearses moving faster."

"That's as may be, Mr Jenkins, but I'm afraid you'll still have to move on. *Please go home.*"

For the first time the officer's voice quivered with a hint of malice.

"Actually, he's protesting, Constable– "

"Sergeant."

"Err, Sergeant... it's a sit-down protest. A peace protest."

"What, *here?*"

"I know. I told him it's ridiculous."

"He's got to be kidding. Belfast City Council... they love peace demonstrations up there. They'd have given him a grant and a patch of lawn outside the City Hall."

"Yes, I know. I suggested something similar. But this is spontaneous, see?"

"And what is your role in all this, Mr Jenkins?"

"Professional interest. I'm a journalist. He called me. I'm covering it for the *Tele*. He says he's got hundreds of others joining him. They're due any minute. There's not much point moving him on now, it'll just get their backs up. They'll be all over the road before you know it. Obstructing the traffic, causing a public nuisance – an affray. Who knows where it could all end?"

"Mmm, I haven't heard anything about this. We normally get notice of demonstrations. These things are usually well organised. Right. Here's what's going to happen. Whilst I'm checking up on this back at the station, you two are going to move along. I'll be through this way later on to make sure you're not here. Right? And let's hope that's an end to it."

Jenkins and Smyth watched the policeman hurry back to his motorcycle, stuff his clipboard into the pannier, mount up and ride off. They looked at each other and shrugged.

"What the hell are you doing, you English twat? I can fight my own battles, thank you very much. You just couldn't resist telling him you're a journalist, could you? And what the hell did you have to go and lie for?"

"Lie? Oh no. I don't think so. Exaggerate, maybe. Anyway,

it'll buy you some time. It'll keep you out of trouble for a while. You don't know who you're taking on when you take on the RUC. They play by their own rules. And they can play very hard and very rough."

Jenkins' portable phone started to ring. The size and weight of a house brick, it distorted the hang of his overcoat.

"Yep... yep. Err-huh... yep. I'm on the Ballyblessington ring road. Yep... about an hour. I think I've found something you'll like. Quirky, but interesting. A human interest/human endurance kind of story... No. No... not at all. I'll fill you in later. McGowan? Err-huh... Mmm... you're right, he can wait for a while. Ok, then. Yep... yep... see you around midday."

Jenkins pressed a few buttons and then struggled to squeeze the portable back into its pocket without tearing the lining.

Smyth shook his head in exasperation.

"My editor. I'm late for work. You know, as much as I'd like to stay here– "

"Look, how many times do I have to tell you, Jenkins, *I don't need your help*, right?"

Jenkins shrugged again, then started to wander off. The dog sat up and barked. Thereupon Jenkins looked round and caught sight of a woman fast approaching from the pavement on the other side of the carriageway, jogging then walking, jogging then walking, red in the face and out of breath.

"What the hell are you doing here?" the flushed-faced woman shouted, as she bore down on Smyth scolding him as if he were a naughty child. "Look at you! Just look at you!"

Smyth ignored her.

"Hello. How do you do. I'm Jenkins, Dillon Jenkins."

Jenkins had stepped into her path and was extending a hand in the manner of a politician canvassing votes. But Peggy Smyth's arms were folded across her chest and weren't for moving.

"Pah! I hope *you're* not encouraging him. What the hell's he doing here, anyway?"

"He's protesting. I was just advising him against it, but he's having none of it."

"Well he's a buck *eejit*, Mr... Mr... Mr Whoever-you-are."

"Jenkins."

"But I'll soon get him moved, Mr Jenkins."

"Mmm, this will be interesting," Jenkins murmured under his breath. He was studying the woman's face. It was strong and angular. Strong bone structure. Vivid blue eyes. Jenkins wasn't sure whether her cheeks were flushed because she'd been rushing or whether she wore a permanent blush. Her colouring was, otherwise, white. Porcelain white. Her hair – strawberry blonde – a mass of curls that tumbled with abandon. It needed brushing. Mid-thirties, he guessed. Unusual, but attractive. Her taste in clothes seemed too old for her – as though she was past caring. Her wardrobe did nothing to flatter what Jenkins imagined to be a curvaceous figure.

"What *are* you doing?" she demanded.

Smyth continued to ignore the commotion, preferring to stare at the pavement beneath his feet.

"He nearly got himself arrested a moment ago."

Smyth looked up and scowled at Jenkins.

"The police? Right, Ignatius, you're coming home with me, right now!" Peggy Smyth growled, growing sterner again.

"Do you know, I don't think he can hear you, Mrs..?"

"Peg... Peggy Smyth."

"Iggy's wife?"

"You kidding? Who'd marry *him*? No, I'm his sister."

"Right, right... sorry. Actually, I was just about to leave. Can I give you a lift anywhere? I'm heading into Fellrock?"

"That would be very nice. Thank you. I'm not going to stay here all day with this daft *eejit*. If you could drop me somewhere near the town, that would be great. I'll see you later, Ignatius, when you've come to your senses."

"I wouldn't count on that," Jenkins muttered, moving off.

Peggy Smyth grunted at her brother and then turned on her

heels to catch up with Jenkins who was already halfway to the car; anxious to get home, showered and fed before he was due at the *Telegraph*.

Ignatius Smyth watched the Zodiac disappear from view from his seat beside the bollard.

The visitors gone, the dog trotted over and lay down at Smyth's feet. Smyth ignored him as he fell into a doze which was repeatedly interrupted by a horn blast or screech of brakes until the rush hour was over.

"Is my brother a lunatic, Mr Jenkins?"

A difficult question. Dillon Jenkins crossed his legs one way and then the other.

"I wouldn't know."

"Ok, if he's not mad, then what's he trying to do?"

Jenkins shrugged. He was unwilling to get dragged into a debate mined with intangibles. He had already allowed himself to get dragged into Peggy Smyth's kitchen against his will. He'd been there for fifteen minutes and there was still no sign of the tea she'd promised him. Jenkins kept looking down at his watch and hoped she'd get the message and let him go.

"And what about you, Mr Jenkins? What are *you* doing here?"

"In Fellrock?"

"Well, in Northern Ireland, I suppose."

"That's a long story."

"Why the hell would anyone want to come and live here?"

"Oh, I don't know. The challenge? It's very different. Anyway, I like it. And, you know, it really is the middle of nowhere. And that's perfect for me at the moment."

"So you do live here, then?"

"Yes."

"Full-time?"

"For now, yes."

"That's a bit drastic."

"I like Northern Ireland. I like the people. They're talkative. Everybody's got a story here. I mean, people won't even make eye contact with you in London these days. I always thought I was a bit mad when I lived there. Like I'd be one of those types who would talk to people at bus stops. You know... the next man in the queue. People don't normally do that in London. I used to get some very strange looks. Like I was crazy or something. But not here. Everybody talks to everybody else. I like that! The country's a talking shop. When I arrived here I realised that I was really quite sane. I think I've found the right asylum, so to speak. Also – as far as my job goes – Northern Ireland's always been one of the most consistent front-line stories. There's no end of news here."

"Is that how you see us, Mr Jenkins? Rich pickings for stories?"

"Well, I don't know– "

"Be honest, Mr Jenkins."

"Dillon."

"Be honest, Dillon."

"I'm a journalist. What do you expect?"

"That's just your job. I think I could tell if you were lying. You're pretty transparent. Your face is very open. I bet you're a terrible liar."

"Maybe."

"Anyway, how do you see us?"

"Troubled."

"Really?"

"Of course."

"Well, I suppose. But don't you get homesick?"

"No."

"Who have you left behind in London?"

"A few friends, some family."

"Large family?"

"Not really. My parents are gone. I've a sister and a handful of cousins."

"Many friends?"

"One or two."

"And, are you married?"

"No. Divorced."

"Oh. Sorry."

"Don't be. It was a long time ago."

"Children?"

"No. No children."

"And how are you about that – about your wife I mean?"

"Hang on, I thought you were going to make– "

"Tea! Oh, God! I'm sorry. I'll forget my head next. Coming right up!"

Peggy dashed to the kettle.

"Tea... I wasn't drinking much tea back then," Jenkins mumbled, sighing and uncrossing his legs.

"When?"

"Before, during and after the divorce."

"Oh, right. When was that, then?"

"Oh, I don't know. Six, seven years ago."

"You ok, now?"

"Now? Sure. Then? No. It all got a bit messy. I was drinking too much. It was quite extreme. It pretty well incapacitated me. The paper I was working on tried to help, but I was too far gone for help then. Things got worse before they got better. That's when I came here. To dry out and start work again."

"And your wife? What happened to her?"

"Oh, she's fine. She remarried. Money, you know."

"But I'm sure it was hard for her too."

"Of course. We were married for about nine years, for God's sake. You'd think we'd been together long enough *then* for her to be able to say hello whenever we run into each other *now*. But I guess she's just bitter."

"Biscuit?"

"Err... ok."

"I hope you like Viscounts."

"Thank you."

"So what happened?"

"Do you really want to know?"

"Only if you want to tell me."

"Not really. I end up giving a slightly different version every time I tell the story."

"Oh never mind then. It's probably got a bit stale by now."

"I'd just say, that when we met, she thought the sun shone out of my arse – if you'll pardon the expression – and by the end she thought, and treated me like I was a complete idiot. I struggled to support her financially. She was used to money and couldn't cope with having to live on a budget."

Jenkins crossed his legs again.

"There must be more to it than that."

"There is. But that's today's version. The sequin that caught the light on the mirrorball tonight... well, this morning."

The conversation stalled.

"Would you like a salad sandwich?" Peggy asked, with eager eyes and placing a warm hand on his forearm.

Jenkins felt threatened by Peggy's physicality and her enthusiasm to slow him down with carbohydrates. It seemed to him that the kitchen was a cobweb, he a fly and Peggy Smyth a rather hungry spider.

8

Lexy Danvers' rise through the ranks of the Loyalist UDC had more to do with his talents as a brawler than for any political nous. He was neither a military tactician, nor a leader of men. His currency was fear and his reputation as a street fighter had earned him a place on the UDC's 'army council' as a provider of muscle to Commander-in-Chief, Marty McGowan. The one needed the other: the sharp mind needed a strong punch.

That Danvers' shaven head was a virgin field – the stubble velvet smooth and unbroken by the plough lines of battle scars – was a testimony to his success as a gladiator. He had proven himself in the arena, unbloodied, unbeaten and unbowed. His skills in close combat were as valued as any of the expensive weaponry smuggled into Northern Ireland in recent times. It was obvious to the elite on the army council how to use him to best effect.

To unleash Danvers on a simple task however, was inadvisable. He was not talented at handling the day-to-day. Lexy Danvers was an all-or-nothing man whose brain didn't function until fired up with a dose of adrenaline sparked by extreme danger or excitement. In an emergency, and once the adrenaline was pumping, Danvers was *the* person to have by your side. He would be the ideal man to send into a burning house to save a child, for instance, in fact any situation which required instinctive reaction and split-second timing.

Like a shark on the prowl, Danvers' brain could respond to danger in nanoseconds. He knew no fear – knew little of anything. Any mundane activity that required forethought, planning or just a moment of concentration was beyond him. To entrust Danvers with the task of delivering the decoy story to Dillon Jenkins of the *Telegraph* therefore, was plain stupidity. Since the outcome of the plan was that Jenkins would be maimed or even executed should the story fail to get into print, it was vital that he received and took note of the misinformation in the first place.

There were to be four authors: McGowan, Danvers and two ageing members of the UDC's paramilitary elite. They had gathered in the smoky side-office of a local community centre in North Belfast to type up the bait.

"If this is going to work, the story's going to need real punch. We're going to have to offer a smoking gun. We're going to have to sacrifice one of our own," Marty McGowan announced grandly to the room.

"A sacrifice?" Lexy queried.

"Yes. A sacrifice. We'll lift someone, get them spiked up with some dodgy chemicals, deliver them round to the peelers, and make sure they've got a few ounces of something or other in their pockets. And Lexy, make sure they can't run away when you bundle them out of the car."

"A sacrificial lamb," Lexy offered, deep in thought.

"Yes. Unfortunate, but it's all in a good cause."

"Ok, what about Jackie Nelson?"

"Too old. He's more your sacrificial mutton. No, doesn't deserve it."

"Ronnie Johnson?"

"Too daft. No one takes that *eejit* seriously enough. No. Vinnie. I think Vinnie's our man."

"Who? Vinnie Wilson?"

"Yeah, Vinnie."

"Vinnie? Are you sure?"

"Yeah."

"Why Vinnie?"

"He's a liability. Short fuse, long neck, deep pockets. I hear he's started a little freelance business. He's been leaning on the community. Diverting funds. Pocketing money. Deserves to be taught a lesson. What do you think lads?"

The two ageing cohorts nodded sagely. They were too old and too wise to disagree with McGowan at this stage – any stage. They viewed the conversation from the sidelines as if watching a game of tennis.

"You sure, Marty?"

"I told you."

"Ok, so it's Vinnie."

"Done!"

Then for the accompanying story. Then writer's block. Blank looks were exchanged. It was incumbent on McGowan to exercise leadership. He smoked, he mused and he thumped the table.

It was McGowan then, who rattled the keys, employing the typing skills he had learned on one of the adult training courses provided for inmates of the Maze Prison. The other three crowded in behind him, looking over his shoulder as he tapped away. The motion of McGowan's index fingers, wagging like water divining rods, transported him back to his days behind bars. Life had been simple then with few responsibilities. He had held a senior rank in the well-ordered hierarchy of the Loyalist block, but in the phoney atmosphere of the prison it was easy to wear the identity of a frustrated military man held captive – a POW – whilst having nothing much to do. His rank though, ensured a regular supply of booze and fags.

The fond memory unwound until the typewriter's ancient ribbon snapped halfway through the second line and in the absence of a spare, the semi-automatic had to be abandoned. Not to be outdone, and determined to complete the job there and then, they transferred into the main hall where they sat down at the long table and began the painstaking task of constructing the communication using the traditional methods of the gangster, which involved the cutting up of the previous week's newspapers, a sheet of A3 paper and a pot of cow gum borrowed from the under-eights' playgroup store cupboard. McGowan finished his first draught in chalk on the blackboard for the other three to copy in sections.

The making of the letter (which they decided was a cultural activity when one of the older men pointed out that he had been producing death threats this way for decades) was lengthy because of all the sticking, but curtailed because the under-eights had used up much of the glue on a *Mutant Ninja Turtles* collage the previous Saturday.

"The Ulster Defence Corps is declaring war on drug traffickers!
The UDC army council will not sanction the selling of drugs in Belfast. We will protect the youth of our community by taking action against those found peddling drugs on our streets.
Vincent Wilson is the first of the scum to be punished. Others will follow and be dealt with more severely. Their activities will be terminated. Terminated with extreme prejudice."

The quote from *Apocalypse Now* was irresistible.

As soon as the note was finished it was put aside to dry whilst the four filed out to the back alley for a fag. Lexy Danvers broke off halfway through to organise Vinnie Wilson's trip to the nearest RUC station. On his return he volunteered to deliver the note which had been folded and placed in a brown manila envelope.

Danvers thought nothing of this task. The instructions were straightforward: "Take the envelope to Jenkins' address in Fellrock, then post it through the letter box." Simple enough, he just had to be sure that Jenkins was not at home at the time of delivery. He did as instructed.

Danvers, however, was unaware of the poor adhesive power of cow gum when challenged by extreme heat. He did not realise that placing the manila envelope on the dashboard of his Rover 2000 in direct sunlight on a hot spring day would result in the cut-out characters curling up and then falling off the paper to which they had been stuck.

As a result, Dillon Jenkins did not know what to make of the sheet of white paper and assortment of loose cut-out letters he found when going through his mail on returning from his overnight stay on the traffic island. Amidst the deluge of junk mail waiting on his doormat that morning, the tatty contents of the brown manila envelope failed to grab his attention and were deposited directly into the kitchen bin. The decoy story would not be appearing in the *Telegraph* as expected. Vinnie Wilson's sacrifice had been in vain.

9

Half a dozen officers were loafing around the walls of the briefing room, taking tentative gulps from plastic vending machine cups; coffee and tea, so foul, so hot and so lacking in any distinctive taste that each sip induced a wince.

"Want another cup, Sam? What's yours? Tea or coffee?" the detective inspector grunted in the direction of one of the other men in dark green, slumped over a filing cabinet in the far corner.

"Does it make any difference, sir?"

"Sausage roll?"

"You kidding?"

The DI fumbled the steaming column of raw sausage meat and soggy pastry towards the wastepaper bin at his feet. His aim was off. The sausage roll flopped over the rim and dripped clear, fatty goo onto the floor. The DI flipped the rest into the bin with the heel of his shoe.

The room resembled a refuge for battered office furniture where the odd mix of desks and filing cabinets appeared to have been arranged to impair access, exit and flow-through: an impenetrable maze of brown formica and grey metal. Though a smoking ban had recently been imposed by the Chief Inspector, the thick layers of nicotine were yet to be covered over with mushroom, cream, magnolia or whatever emulsion paint the office manager happened to have lurking in his store cupboard.

"Ok, quieten down!" the DI barked to summon the attention of the detective constables dangling around the walls like last year's Christmas decorations.

No one looked up, the murmuring continuing unabated.

"Right you lot!" the DI tried again, raising his voice and clapping his hands. "Murdoch, get that effing sarnie into your face before I ram it up your arse!"

DI Williams knew the language his people understood best.

Attention drawn, the DI worked through the latest list of break-ins, muggings and car thefts and was about to do his wrap-up when he remembered the man on the roundabout.

"Oh yes, and we've a spot of bother on the Fellrock road," DI Williams continued in his clipped 'briefing' speak; a way of talking that even those with the shortest of attention spans could follow. "Sit-down protest. Ballyblessington ring road. Fellrock turn-off. A solo effort. One bloke on his own. So far, no hassle. Potential for a larger disturbance though. Billy?"

"Sir?"

"What do we do?"

"*Wha?*"

"Exactly, Billy. How the hell can you follow what's going on if you're staring out of the effing window?"

The temptation to hurl a piece of chalk, cheese, a sausage roll or anything to get his officer's attention was pressing, but then, as Williams well knew, he was a detective inspector, not a schoolteacher. Same difference, he thought.

"Right then. Traffic branch have been down there. Hang on... Sergeant!" DI Williams bellowed out the door. The motorcycle policeman ambled into the briefing room.

"Sir?"

"Sergeant... Fellrock road. What's going on?"

"The protest? There's only one man there now. A Mr Smyth. But it seems he's attracting attention. He's already found a sidekick. A journalist. They're protesting for peace. Or that's what they're saying. They don't seem like they could be much of a danger to anyone but themselves. The journalist claims that they have support arriving in numbers at any time, but I doubt it. It's more the trouble they could attract from passers-by and they're a distraction to drivers, a traffic hazard."

"Exactly, Sergeant. They're not a threat to anyone, it's more the trouble they *could* attract. If we let them sit there too long, you can be sure there will be other idiots who will want to follow their lead. If it is a genuine peace campaign we all know how they can get out of hand, especially when the campaigners start marching. Ok, so what do we do?"

DI Williams leaned forward looking for raised hands. No one in the room was *that* stupid.

"Anyone?" he asked again, leaning even further forward.

"We're going to have to make life a little awkward for them. Make them more uncomfortable than they probably are already," he added.

"Knock them about a bit?"

"No, Frank, this isn't the effing seventies. Look, I am expecting this thing to fizzle out quickly. I *want* this thing to fizzle out quickly. So let's just make sure it does."

Williams looked round the room taking in the expressions of each of his men in turn. Thank God they issue them with a uniform and a gun, he thought to himself when he realised what a gormless-looking bunch they were. Few, if any, possessed drive. Most looked as if they were killing time till the end of their shifts and home. Williams couldn't remember being this lethargic when he was in the lower ranks. He blamed himself though. It was his job to motivate his men.

"Simmonds."

"Sir?"

"Get some background on the local man. Err, what's his name, Sergeant?"

"Smyth, sir. Ignatius Smyth."

"And the other one, the journalist?"

"Dillon Jenkins. A reporter at the *Telegraph*, I believe, sir."

"Right. I want to put a stop to this before it takes off. We do not, repeat *not*, want an effing peace campaign on our hands. Let's get this over with – however, whoever, whatever."

10

By midday the flow of traffic had eased on the Ballyblessington bypass. Cars moved freely across the junction at the Fellrock turn-off. It was still necessary for drivers to slow on the approach from the coast road and stop beside the island before joining the dual carriageway, but they had no time to admire the view of Ignatius Smyth sitting by the bollard. He was ignored by most and preferred it that way.

There were few passers-by on foot. There had been three all morning: a postman, a pensioner walking a dog and a pregnant teenager pushing a pram. They gave him a wide berth. Smyth looked pretty startling sprawled on the ground in his scruffy overalls; his uncombed hair – a matted black thatch; his face and hands dirty from sitting by the roadside. A closer inspection would have observed his deep blue eyes, but few would dare approach. It seemed to Smyth that no one in Ballyblessington cared to walk anywhere any more anyway. There was nowhere to walk to along the dual carriageway that couldn't be accessed by car and nowadays everyone had at least one, if not two or three.

Smyth rubbed his temples, his head still fuzzy from the whiskey. It was a relief to know that nothing was required of him but to sit and let the day drift by.

For the first two or three hours he entertained himself by trying to guesstimate the passing of time. First he tried a minute. He counted the seconds in his head and then checked his wristwatch when he thought the sixty seconds had passed. *One elephant, two elephants, three elephants...* He found he was out by five seconds. Next he tried counting five minutes in his head and found himself out by thirty seconds. Then he tried to guesstimate half an hour by intuition alone – the counting was starting to drive him mad – but was delighted to find that he was only twenty seconds out. He then had a go at an hour, but got bored and gave up.

He moved onto gambling, choosing to bet on the frequency of buses. A bus would have to appear before twenty cars came by. If twenty cars passed around the roundabout before an Ulsterbus came along, then he would lose the bet and have to pay the forfeit of a limb. On the first twenty cars he staked his left leg. On the next twenty cars he gambled the right. By the time an Ulsterbus *did* come crawling by – about another hour later – he had hypothetically lost both legs, all his fingers, both hands, an arm, both ears and his nose.

Tired of homespun entertainment, he decided to take a nap and was just dropping off to sleep when something landed with a thud on the bollard behind him.

"What kind of blithering idiot are you, Iggy?"

"Shit, you made me jump!"

"Well, I've brought you some lunch. Though don't ask me why," Peggy Smyth said, brandishing a bulging carrier bag over her brother's head.

"Actually, I'm starving. What did you bring?"

"Just some sandwiches, though you don't deserve anything."

"No, no... thanks, you're an angel."

"I know. And I don't suppose you'll be home for your tea?"

"Can't."

"Can't or won't?"

"Just can't."

"That's ok, but don't forget there's bills to pay."

He ignored her. Nothing new.

"Bloody hell, Iggy. What is it with you? Don't you even have the manners to say 'thank you'?"

"I said 'thank you'. *Thank you*," Smyth murmured.

It was too late. Peggy dumped the bag of food on top of the bollard and spun round to stomp back up the road.

"We'll see how long you can keep this up!" she shouted, goose-stepping towards Fellrock.

Smyth waited for her to turn the corner before seizing the carrier bag and making an assault on the contents. The sensation of warm bacon on his taste buds made him drool. He ate fast, driven by intense hunger. He rammed the food into his mouth, his fingers dancing like piano keys on each mouthful, shovelling in the next before the previous one had been swallowed. He was overjoyed that his sister had thought to pack a litre bottle of water – a cure for the headache setting in.

During the feeding frenzy the mongrel trotted back, attracted by the scent of the meat. It sat at Smyth's feet and looked across at him with sad eyes.

"You can go and find your own bloody lunch, mate. You're not having any of mine. Go on, *Geet!*" Smyth sneered.

The dog slid onto its stomach, lying down with its paws outstretched and trying to look disinterested. It rested its snout on the pavement and glanced up with a wistful expression.

"It's no use looking at me like that, you stupid mutt."

There was something human about the dog's demeanour that got Smyth thinking of reincarnation. He could imagine the dog as a grubby urchin, hanging around a street corner in Rio.

If reincarnation were possible, what animal, he wondered, would he be coming back as? Probably something insignificant like plankton. What would he come back as if he had the choice? Easy: a blue whale. Strong and powerful with a two hundred year life cycle.

"Hey! What were you in a former life?" Smyth asked the dog, throwing it a corner of sandwich.

As afternoon gave way to evening, Ignatius Smyth sat contemplating. It was hot and getting hotter. There was no breeze and the humidity was building. Smyth longed for rain. Shortly after dark it came in a sudden cloudburst. Unexpected.

As unexpected as rain can ever be in Ireland. Smyth had smelt it just before sundown. There was a moistness in the air he had mistaken for the coming dew, but within an hour came a pitter-pattering on the tarmac. Within seconds it had accelerated from a light drumming into a torrent that soaked through to the skin.

As the cloudburst intensified, Smyth wrapped his arms around his shins and gathered his legs in under him, tucking his head into his lap and curling into a ball. The black cloud above had moved in quickly; the rain would fall in sheets and then pass by.

Smyth shivered as rainwater dripped down the back of his neck – oddly refreshing. Despite the rain he felt relaxed and comfortable enough, and as his eyes started to flicker he dozed off into a light sleep.

Smyth didn't know whether it was the clap of thunder or the sudden jolting that awoke him. But no sooner was he awake than he was conscious of being heaved to his feet by hands grasping at his overalls and jerking the seam at the crotch hard into his groin.

Voices were barking orders that he couldn't decipher.

"In the van! Get him into the van, now!"

Seized by the arms, Smyth watched the ground speed by beneath him. His head was being forced down onto his breastbone by a strong hand, his toes burned as they bobbed along the concrete, flailing behind him like tin cans on a wedding car. His vision was framed by the thrashing black legs frogmarching him along the pavement in a blur and the thickset arms that had him clamped by the wrists and shoulders and dragging him like a sack of potatoes.

Suddenly the world seemed to spin away from him as he tumbled through the air, crash-landing onto a hard floor, which his fumbling fingertips detected to be corrugated metal. A van floor. There was a strong smell of diesel laced with the scent of fried food and a hint of methane.

The doors clunked shut and an engine coughed into life. He was thrown backwards by the sudden acceleration. Looking up he could see the backs of two heads silhouetted in the cab window. The rain roared onto the roof and side panels.

As soon as Smyth regained his balance he sat up and pressed his face against the rear window and watched as the island shrank from view. Through the early morning gloom he could make out the dog. It was barking. He could see the mouth moving, but couldn't hear the sound. And just as the island disappeared, he caught a glimpse of a Ford Zodiac passing on the other side of the carriageway.

Bloody Jenkins, he thought. *Where the hell were you when I needed you?*

Jenkins cursed. Hated rain. He hated sun, wind, ice, snow, sleet, hail, mist, fog and cloud in equal measure. In fact, he hated weather of any description. He didn't see the police van as it sped past. There was nothing to distinguish it. No siren. No flashing lights. And anyway, visibility was poor in the thunderstorm.

He had spent another exhausting day struggling to produce a follow-up to his unpublished feature on the drugs scene. His heart hadn't been in the job and he wondered if he cared enough. Maybe a drugs culture in Belfast was better than one based on bombs and bullets. Maybe it would bring some relief – an antidote to war. No, just more misery for a population preyed upon by extremists and neglected by government.

Montgomery's attitude didn't help either. The editor's cynicism dissipated Jenkins' enthusiasm for the job and encouraged the kind of lethargy that leads to writer's block.

As Jenkins passed by the roundabout on his way home to Fellrock, he had assumed he would see Smyth. He had spent much of his journey from Belfast speculating as to how the tyre fitter would be coping in the rain. Jenkins was disappointed therefore, when he found the island deserted – disappointed to be proved right about Smyth and Smyth's stamina in the face of bad weather.

"So he couldn't stick it for more than forty-eight hours, eh? Never mind," he sighed.

Sadly, it reaffirmed Jenkins' belief in the shallow and self-serving nature of man.

A pang of loneliness struck him till he caught a glimpse of the dog trotting back onto the island, the cloudburst over. The dog started to yelp; front paws hopping in the air with every bark, splashing in the puddles and jumping round like a clockwork toy.

Jenkins pulled off the road and turned down a narrow farm track to the left, just after the junction at the top of the Fellrock road. His tyres spun on the grass threatening to get him bogged down. He made sure to change up into third and kept the accelerator steady. Thirty yards up the track he pulled over onto what felt like firm ground and yanked on the handbrake.

As Jenkins walked back to the island, the dog sat up and then ran towards him, its tail wagging like a metronome.

"Hey there!" Jenkins said, bending to pat the dog and pulling at its ears.

"Where's that idiot in the overalls, hey? Did you take a bite? Chase him away? You haven't eaten him have you?"

The dog settled. Jenkins stood back and searched his coat pockets for a plastic bag. He found one from his lunchtime sandwich, tore it open, spread it across the tarmac, sat down and leaned back against the bollard. The dog lay alongside, its head resting on Jenkins' lap. The streets were drying fast; the fallen water turning to steam.

Jenkins thanked God the rain had stopped. *Rain's the Devil's work*, his grandad would say.

There's no such thing as the Devil, it's just God when he's drunk... The Tom Waits lyric made him laugh more.

Sleep came quickly.

11

Ignatius Smyth's face was creased with lines. Asleep, he had tumbled onto the cell floor from the bed: a concrete perch – cold and narrow. A rude awakening.

Dazed, he sat on the floor staring up at the new day visible through the skylight. During the night an emaciated mattress and pillow had been his only comforts; the pillowcase stained yellow by many oily scalps. It was a miracle that he had been able to sleep at all and defy gravity until the morning.

In a former life Ballyblessington RUC Station had been a Georgian town house. It now resembled a miniature Fort Knox. Few of the exterior Georgian features were visible under the steel mesh and corrugated cladding installed to protect those inside from those out. It stood in the town centre, halfway down the high street, but wire netting fixed high along the top of the fencing ensured it was more than just a stone's throw away.

The local police were now so heavily protected against those fellow citizens of murderous intent, that they lived in isolation – not least whilst on duty – and had become remote figures, cocooned behind metal plate, bulletproof glass and Kevlar.

The inside of the building was not unlike that of any police station found anywhere in Britain or Ireland. An interior characterised by outmoded furniture, the bouquet of bleach, a palette of blue and grey paint and posters warning of pickpockets, bag snatchers, sneak thieves, bogus callers and muggers and/or of the perils of driving too fast, too tired or too drunk. And unique to Northern Ireland there was also a poster urging those in the know to supply information that might lead to the arrest of terrorists – a confidential telephone line for the shopping of friends and neighbours.

In contrast to the serious business of the exterior fortifications, the reception area usually purveyed informality. A well-rehearsed comedy: *Z-Cars* with laughs; a front of house niceness to mask the grim business conducted backstage.

Since daybreak the flow of customers had increased from a drip dripping of ones and twos to an early morning trickle. Ignatius Smyth's arrival in the middle of the night had been chaotic – a struggle whose ripples were felt throughout the station. To an institution whose belief in 'control' was absolute, 'order' was the desired ambience for the workplace and so the commotion was dealt with promptly – Smyth bundled into a cell, the door slammed and calm restored.

The officer on duty at the front desk wore the demeanour of well-trained politeness, but the station sergeant had appeared from the offices behind to handle a specific query with a scowl.

"Are you going to take the damn photo or not?"

The sergeant was in full flow.

"You know I can't."

"Goddamn it, Tulley, I dream of the day when mine isn't the only head stuck up above the frigging parapet! So why did you come in here if you're not going to take the bloody photo? And what the hell are you doing here at this unearthly hour?"

"To avoid a fuss. And, and to explain... to explain and apologise," Brendan Tulley stuttered.

As editor of the local paper Tulley should have been used to working under pressure, but the RUC could be unpredictable and, he knew, possibly prejudiced against his kind. There was also a sinister glint in the sergeant's eyes that made Tulley feel vulnerable.

"*Apologise* so I wouldn't give you a hard time, I suppose?"

"No, no, not at all. I just thought it polite. I know you wouldn't give me a hard time, Sergeant," Tulley lied.

"Exactly, Tulley. We're not the Gestapo. Anyway, sod your politeness!" the station sergeant hissed. "All we are asking for is a photo of our second fifteen to put up in the frigging canteen. I wouldn't call that collusion. The paras aren't going to shoot you for that."

"Yes. Yes, of course. But you know how it is. It's just– "

"Just what?"

Luckily for Tulley, the station sergeant's concentration was broken by the entrance of a man in grey and white pinstripes. They watched as he struggled through the small gap he had prised open between the swing doors at the front of the station. First an arm, then a leg. Long, pipe-cleaner limbs that made his head look oversized – like an escapee from a Lowry painting. Hunched.

"Yes?" the sergeant asked, unsure whether to smile or scowl and attempting both through gritted teeth.

"Mr Craddick for Mr Smyth. His solicitor," the man announced in a whining voice that was hard on the ears. He handed a business card to the sergeant.

"Does he *really* need you?" the sergeant enquired.

"He asked for a solicitor. He seems to think so."

"Did he call you himself?"

"No, he called his sister late last night, then she called me. Said he was extremely agitated. She sounded concerned about the situation. I phoned here immediately."

"Here?"

"Here. Just to make sure he was all right. But he was asleep by then. I said I'd drop by at around this time. You weren't expecting me?"

"No. Err, maybe, Mr?"

"Craddick."

"Let's see now. Craddick... Mr Craddick for Mr Smyth. Well, there's no note about you here, Mr Craddick," the sergeant said, scanning the station's giant occurrence book and then scowling at the duty officer.

"Typical! Nevertheless, may I see my client?"

"Sure. Take a seat for a moment," the station sergeant replied, waving towards the wooden bench bolted against the wall opposite. The sergeant started to move off in search of Smyth, but then hesitated, suddenly remembering the journalist, who was wandering off towards the front entrance.

"Tulley! Wait there! I'll be right back!" the sergeant shouted, nodding to the duty officer to be alert before leaving the room.

Tulley followed Craddick over to the bench as directed.

"Trouble?" Tulley asked, leaning towards Craddick so he could whisper into the man's ear; a stab at discretion.

Craddick ignored him.

"You in trouble?" Tulley persisted.

"That's no business of yours, sir."

The solicitor, already tense, recoiled from Tulley like a tortoise retracting into its shell.

"Tulley," Tulley said, offering his hand.

"Ugh?"

"Brendan Tulley, the *Ballyblessington Spectator*."

Silence.

"Brendan Tulley, the *Ballyblessington Spectator*."

Again silence.

"And you are?"

A pause.

"Craddick."

"Craddock?"

"No. Crad-dick."

"Agh. *Dick* not *Dock*."

"Exactly." Craddick groaned, raising his eyebrows.

"And?"

"And what, Mr Tulley?"

"You: trespassing? Aggravated burglary? Buggery? Assault and battery? Unpaid parking ticket?"

73

"I'm a solicitor, Mr Tulley!"

"Oh, right... pinstripes, briefcase, serious expression. Who are you waiting for?"

"My client, Mr Tulley. And I am not at liberty to tell you any more than you can discover by observing events from that seat. So please don't be asking me any further questions."

The station sergeant reappeared to rescue Craddick from his tormentor.

"This way, Mr?"

"THE NAME'S CRADDICK!"

"I'll take you to your client now," the sergeant said impassively, beckoning him to follow.

Tulley stood up.

"Tulley, sit!" the sergeant bellowed.

Tulley sat. The duty officer bristled.

Craddick meanwhile, passed under the sergeant's arm which was arching over him to hold open the swing door at the rear of the desk. Craddick's footsteps told of a slow walk down a long corridor which Tulley imagined was lined with cells.

"Ah, Mr Smyth. Good morning. I hear you've been rather inconvenienced," Craddick said, walking into the cell furthest from reception. He approached his client, lounging on the concrete bed, and stood over him, his hands clasped on the briefcase that dangled between his legs like a sporran.

In the course of AJ Craddick's career his firm had defended men and women of all political persuasions and of all criminal tendencies. Some had been innocent. Many not. He didn't judge. He thought the law like chess and his cases chess games to be won. His application of the rules of the game was a means to an end – a strategy to win. He rarely minded whether his clients were innocent or guilty; he only cared that they told *him* the truth.

A gangly man; years of leaning on one arm in court – a slouch, designed to convey confidence to both judge and jury –

had led to a stoop; this, over many years, had evolved into a hunch. His head now curled down to rest against his left shoulder which ensured that eye contact was kept to a minimum.

Craddick's was no nine-to-five occupation. His job was his vocation, his *raison d'être* – the love of his life.

In the reception area of the police station, meanwhile, boredom was setting in. Tulley was staring at his feet whilst contemplating running away, but wouldn't dare risk it.

"Now, where were we? *Tulley!*" the station sergeant barked on his return behind the counter and startling Tulley out of his daydream.

"What's with the solicitor, Sergeant?" Tulley asked, gingerly.

"Never you mind."

"No, seriously."

"He's just checking up on some nutter we took in last night. A bit of a troublemaker, allegedly. It's nothing, really."

"What kind of trouble, Sergeant?"

"None. Now you keep your nose out, Tulley. That's not why you're here– "

"Has he been charged with anything?"

"I don't actually know. I wasn't on duty. I don't think so."

"What's he done?"

"Why the hell should I tell you?"

"Your photo."

"What about my photo?"

"I've been thinking about it."

"What?"

"Maybe I could send somebody down. But discreetly. You understand what I mean, don't you? I know you do– "

"Yes, yes. Of course."

"Ok. So, who's the guy? What's he done?"

"Well, Mr Craddick's client has been a bit of a naughty boy, Brendan."

Just then Craddick reappeared with Ignatius Smyth. Craddick contorted his face into a scowl, which provoked a lingering silence.

"If you're not charging my client, I take it that we're free to leave?" Craddick asked with a calm detachment.

The two policemen at the desk conferred briefly, which culminated in a nod in Craddick's direction.

"Have a word with him, Mr Craddick. We don't want to see your client in here again," the sergeant added.

"But– "

"But, yes. He's free to go, for now. And please – remind him of his responsibilities."

More nods. Craddick shuffled Smyth out of the building before minds were changed.

The two RUC men turned to converse whilst Tulley stared through the frosted safety glass doors, watching Craddick and Smyth as they crossed the yard heading for the security gates.

"So what did that guy do, exactly?" Tulley called over to the sergeant.

"What about the photo?"

"When's your next game?"

"Saturday."

"Who are you playing?"

"Shorts."

"Where?"

"Holywood Road, East Belfast."

"What time?"

"Two-thirty kick off."

"Ok, I'll get somebody down at two. But don't be expecting any coverage in the paper, mind."

"Look, Tulley, I don't want you to print anything about it in your bloody nationalist rag. Am I stupid? It's the last match of the season. I just want you to organise a team photo to go on the wall of our frigging canteen."

"Ok, ok. No problem. Now, what did you say that man

Smyth has done?"

"Nothing."

"Then why the fuss?"

"He's a nuisance."

"Yeah, but what sort of nuisance?"

"He's been involved in starting up some kind of demo. A peace protest on the ring road, I believe. I don't know, sounds nuts to me."

"Sounds interesting."

"I assure you it's not. And don't you be getting involved. We've sent him home. Let's hope he stays there."

"Yeah, maybe I should pay him a visit. As stories go it beats the brawl at the youth club disco last week and the cat up the tree in Ballyholme."

"Keep out of it, Tulley. We don't need you getting him all excited, photo or no."

But Tulley was already out the door. He had watched the shadows of Smyth and his solicitor dissolve into the distance and was of a mind to follow. Out on the street the morning sun blazed onto the RUC station and into Tulley's eyes. He shielded his face and scanned the length of the road for signs of Craddick and – *what was his name?* Then spotted them in the far corner of the NCP car park opposite, where they were clambering into a green Rover. They drove off towards the exit, Craddick behind the wheel. Tulley's attempt to wave them down went unseen. Having passed through the barrier, the Rover disappeared into the distance heading for the ring road.

"Bugger!" Tulley swore under his breath.

12

Dillon Jenkins was a slow waker. Monday to Friday his alarm was set for seven. When it rang, it was ignored, Jenkins turning a deaf ear and lying under the covers for another half an hour, devoid of enthusiasm and wracked with guilt. He would wait for the burst of energy that would enable him to leap out from under the duvet and embrace the day with a smile. It never came. His extraction from bed, like the pulling of a rotten molar, was always stubborn and painful.

The second morning on the roundabout and Jenkins opened his eyes to a clear sky; conscious of his whereabouts from the first spark of being awake. He felt vulnerable out in the open; disturbed by the hypothermia gnawing at his bones, the hardness of the pavement and the dust blown up by the traffic. In place of the seven o'clock alarm, a foot was tapping at his calves, and then from above came a familiar voice.

"Jenkins... Jenkins wake up, you *eejit!* What the hell are you doing here? Jenkins... Jenkins!"

This was lie-in hell.

"Hey, Smyth! Go easy, man! Go easy!"

Jenkins sat up, ruffled his hair, glanced at his watch – Goddamn it! it was half seven already – and looked about him, yawning. He welcomed the sun as it thawed his face. It would soon be warm. But then, there was Ignatius Smyth bearing down on him and barking.

"Hey, Jenkins! What the– "

"Gentle, gentle. Be gentle, Smyth. I hardly slept a wink. Anyway, where the hell have you been?"

"Och, never mind me. What are you doing here?" Smyth countered, then surrendering to Jenkins' evasiveness with a sigh, sat down and leaned against the bollard. He tried a change of mood: quiet and contemplative.

Jenkins tempted him with a cigarette from a soggy pack, hoping a smoke would calm him down. The cigarette looked antique. Smyth shook his head.

"Well, Dillon?"

"Well, what?"

"Well, what are you doing here?"

"Oh, I don't know. I guess I only meant to sit down for a minute and then I just kind of dozed off. And then before I know it, you're standing there kicking at me. Anyway, what happened to you? Sneak off home for a good night's sleep?"

"Taken into custody."

"The police?"

"Who else?"

"The copper on the bike?"

"Didn't see him."

"Did they charge you?"

"Just a caution."

"You were lucky. And do you think that that's it, then? I mean, do you think they'll let you carry on? Err... are you going to carry on?"

"Of course I'm going to carry on. And no, I don't think they will let me, but they're going to have a fight on their hands to try and stop me."

Jenkins paused to take a long drag.

"You all right, Smyth?"

"They tried to put the wind up me, but I'm ok. It'll take more than that. Anyway, I'm here, aren't I? And what about you? What the hell are you doing here? Hadn't you better get off to work?"

"Well, let's face it – in a way I am."

"What?"

"At work. I'm a journalist. And I told you; you interest me. You might only be worth a line or two now, a paragraph at most, but maybe you'll grow up to be front page news one day."

Smyth stared at the ground.

"Thanks very much!" he said, broodily. "Is that why you're here?"

There followed a long silence; Jenkins holding his breath, whilst Smyth glared into space.

"Fuck you!" Smyth suddenly shouted, springing to his feet and stomping off towards the roundabout.

"Oh, come on! What the hell is it now?" Jenkins called out after him, struggling to get up and swaying when the blood rushed to his head.

"Fuck you! Fuck you!" Smyth cursed over his shoulder.

"My God, you've got one hell of a short fuse! You shouldn't take me so bloody seriously."

Smyth spun round and came lurching back towards Jenkins, eyes blazing.

"Look, this *is* pretty damn serious! People have died. I warn you, you'd better not be investing your time here in column inches. You're either for me or against me in this. If this is just another story to you, then you can bugger off right now."

"Oh, come on, man. For heaven's sake, calm down. For a peacenik, Smyth, you've got a bloody evil temper! Of course I'm 'for you' or I wouldn't be standing here shouting at you now, would I?"

"Wouldn't you? What *are* you doing here, anyway? I didn't ask for your help."

"Yeah, you've made that perfectly clear, but maybe there's stuff I can help you with. I do have a certain expertise."

"Look, I don't need your kind of help. Got it?"

The shouting was drawing the attention of commuters at the junction. They couldn't hear the arguing for engine noise, but it was easy to see what was going on from Smyth's gesticulations.

Jenkins made a tactical withdrawal, wandering off towards the middle of the roundabout, puffing on the cigarette stuck to his bottom lip and taking staccato steps to save his trouser bottoms from the dewy grass. Out of the corner of his eye he watched as Smyth started to trudge slow circles around him.

Jenkins stopped, folded his arms and stared; pensive – like a football manager, stranded on the sidelines and helpless, as his players abandon team tactics.

Smyth, keeping to the outside edge of the roundabout, was just completing his second circuit when he looked up to see a short dumpy man jogging into view from the Fellrock road. Judging by his heavy breathing, pained expression and style of dress – a three-button two-piece – he was no jogger.

Jenkins glanced up as the man crossed onto the traffic island and headed straight for them. He was ashen-faced and overheating, and as he approached, Jenkins noticed that the back of the man's hand, clasping an A4 notepad, was covered in dark hair. Jenkins thought of Biffo the Bear in the *Beano*. As he neared, the man slowed to walking pace.

Jenkins looked over to Ignatius Smyth for a reaction. Smyth frowned in apprehension.

Jenkins noticed how shabby Smyth's appearance had become, not improved by a night in the cells – his blue overalls were grubbier than ever and his face obscured by dark stubble.

"Hello, Mr..?" the visitor prompted, stepping up to Ignatius Smyth on the edge of the roundabout, and panting through a forced smile.

"What's it to you?" Smyth replied abruptly, burying his hands in his pockets.

"I'm from the *Ballyblessington Spectator*. I was in the RUC station just before. I saw you leaving. You're Mr Smyth, aren't you?"

"So why ask if you know?"

"Manners."

"What?"

"I mean, it's good manners to get someone's name right. That's all."

"So, what do you want, Mr..?"

"Tulley. I'm Brendan Tulley."

"So, what do you want, Mr. Tulley?"

"The police told me about your campaign. I'd like to get a story in Thursday's paper for you, if you're agreeable, Mr Smyth. Maybe get a photographer down. You know."

"Do you really think your readers are going to be interested in me?" Smyth replied, wearily.

"Yes, absolutely. I think our readers will be very interested in your camp– "

"It's a protest."

"Sorry... 'protest'. I can't promise that they'll want to support you, but they'll be interested all right. For a start they'll be concerned about the amount of disruption that the protest might cause and whether they will be inconvenienced by it. The locals hate traffic jams."

"I can't see how my sitting here's going to inconvenience anybody."

"That's the spirit. Well, have you got time to talk to me now?"

"I don't know about that. I'm not really up to it right now. You could do worse than to speak to Mr Jenkins over there, though. He seems to know everything there is to know about anything – or thinks he does."

"Ok. But who is he?"

"He's press, like you. Or so he tells me. Works on the *Tele*."

"A reporter? Oh dear. Don't tell me someone's got here before me."

"Don't worry. Mr Jenkins is only here as a helper. He gives me advice. Not that I ever take it. Talk to him. He knows the story. I'll just need to have a word with him first. Hang on, wait here a minute."

Smyth strolled over to Jenkins, who had been watching from the middle of the roundabout.

"It's the *Specky*. They want an interview," Smyth said in a hushed voice.

"What! With *you*?"

"No, Idi-Bloody-Amin."

"Look, before you go rushing off to talk to him, Smyth, I want to clear one or two things up. Firstly, if I was going to sell you out, I would have done it by now and secondly– "

"Look, I know, I know. You're worried about losing your scoop– "

"For God's sake, Smyth! Please understand one thing. You're interesting, but not *that* interesting. I've got plenty of other stories to follow up. I don't need yours. It's only of local interest, anyway. Go and talk to that man, for God's sake. He'll give you better coverage than the *Telegraph* and who knows? Let's face it, if this thing takes off, the *Ballyblessington Spectator* will be just the start. The rest of the media will be down here in droves then, believe me."

"Please, God. No!"

"Look, you *eejit*. It's exactly what you need. It'll get your point across. It'll bring you some support. It might also keep the police at bay for a while."

"Ok, ok. I hear what you're saying. Look, I was thinking... why don't you talk to him for me?"

"Me? Why the hell would I want to do that?"

"'Cos you said you wanted to help me and 'cos you know what to say. I'd be useless. I'm not diplomatic. You said it... I need to talk to the press. Well, maybe *I* can't speak the language... but *you* can. You could do it for me. You could do it standing on your head."

"And what do I get out of this?"

"Hang on! You were the one who said you wanted to help. Well, here you are... help! Start by talking to this guy. If *you* think it's that important, *you* handle it."

"You mean you're actually asking *me* to represent *you*... to be your spokesman?"

"Well, if you put it that way... yes. Why not, if it keeps you and them out of my hair? Yeah. Why not? Yes, you can be my press spokesman."

"God! Aren't I the lucky one? I take it that this is some kind of promotion, then?"

"Don't build your part."

"You know Smyth, you really are a great motivator."

Smyth shrugged.

"Ok then. If you're sure that's what you want, I'll go and talk to this clown."

Jenkins gave a thumbs up and marched over towards Tulley.

"Mr. Jenkins?" Tulley said, grasping Jenkins' hand with enthusiasm.

"Shall we get down to business, Mr... Mr?"

"Tulley. Brendan Tulley. *Ballyblessington Spectator.*"

"Yes, Mr Tulley. Fire away."

"Off the record, Mr Jenkins– "

"Dillon."

"Off the record, Dillon, what's the score with this guy?"

"Good question."

"Is he on the level?"

"I would like to say 'yes', but, I'm not really sure."

"So what's your angle? Why're you here?"

"Another good question. I'm not sure about that either, I'm afraid. And that's the truth of it."

"I mean, are you covering this for the *Tele*? Is this a story for you?"

"Well, as you know, we're capable of making a story out of almost anything, Mr Tulley."

"Yes. But you know what I mean, Dillon. *Is* there really a story in what this man's up to or not?"

"For me? I have my doubts. For you? Certainly. It's good

local news. And one thing I would say for sure is that *if* he stays here long enough and *if* he refuses to budge, the police aren't going to like it and then things could get interesting."

"Right, ok. Look, I know this is going to be a bit awkward, but I need to take you through the 'who, where, what, why and when'," Tulley said, flapping open his notepad.

"No problem," Jenkins replied, staring at Tulley's hairy sausage-like fingers wrapped round the open book. "Actually," Jenkins continued, "I think your story will help him. It'll legitimise what he's doing. It'll help articulate a valid reason for his sitting here."

"Why? Are you suggesting that this *isn't* a peace protest?"

"*He* definitely seems to think so. He says it is, but I've spoken to his sister and she has her doubts."

"And what about you? Do you buy into this?"

"Look, as I say, I'm not really sure what he's up to, Brendan. But, even though he annoys the hell out of me – and me him, for that matter – there's just something about him that draws you in and makes you want to help, whatever the cause or reason."

"I guess that's a maybe, then?"

Jenkins offered a smile.

"More than a maybe."

"Ok, Dillon. That was off the record. Now let's take this from the top," Tulley said, asserting himself and cuing the commencement of the interview by waving his pen like a baton.

"Fire away."

"His name?"

"Smyth. Ignatius Smyth."

"Occupation?"

"Tyre fitter. He lives and works in Fellrock."

"Why has he taken to sitting on this traffic island?"

"It's a sit-down protest for peace, in response to the Antrim Road shooting..."

Absorbed by the journalists' discussion, Smyth was startled when he felt a hand tap him on the shoulder.

"God, Peggy!"

"Brought some soup."

She passed him a Thermos flask.

"Oh, right. Thanks."

They linked arms and stood and watched the journalists.

Smyth was suddenly gripped with a sense of foreboding that, like the throwing of a message in a bottle out to sea, his story was about to escape the island.

13

A football soared past Marty McGowan's head. A seven-year-old followed, chasing after the ball and brushing by at knee height, arms pumping. McGowan arched an eyebrow.

Two teams of kids in blue or red football shirts chittered whilst waiting for the ball's return for a throw-in. Somewhere in the tangle of nylon stood McGowan's youngest boy. Marty McGowan kept losing sight of him in the crowd; the miniature players looking so alike. Same kit, same haircuts.

The pitch – a spring-hardened patch with worn-to-mud goalmouths – was a close-cropped oasis amidst two acres of grass lightly mined with dog turds. The playing fields were north of the city, above the Shankill in Woodvale Park. Both teams of fledgling footballers had been transported there by excitable parents who now faced each other across the pitch in two battle lines, hands in pockets and throats sore from shouting encouragement and abuse.

"Take him on son, take him on! That's it, that's it son. Now lay it off... lay it off!"

Marty McGowan was shouting louder than most.

"Ok! So where is our story, Lexy? What the fuck is Jenkins up to?"

McGowan was shouting football and whispering business whilst shaking a scrunched-up copy of the *Telegraph* in his fist.

"Maybe we missed it, Marty."

McGowan was on the verge of rage. He had started the day feeling irritated, but was now passing through angry at speed.

Rage – Lexy Danvers knew – could be next and would result in some serious harm coming to someone, anyone, somewhere, anywhere; maybe to him. It was a while since McGowan had inflicted a physical punishment himself – he had others to do that now – but in a rage, he was unpredictable. And should a Stanley knife come to hand, he could slice a nose open or an ear off in a flash.

Danvers was practising his diplomatic skills in a sweat.

"How the hell could we miss it, Lexy? It's a major story – front bloody page news. It wasn't like Linfield beating the Glens, or the weather forecast. It wouldn't be buried in births, deaths and bloody marriages."

"So what are you saying, Marty?"

"You know what I'm saying, Lexy, you tube!"

"What?"

"You know, Danvers!"

"Ok. So he has something on us?"

"Too fecking right. Why else didn't he print our bloody story?"

"So you think he knows about the imports?"

"Can't be sure, Lexy. I want to say no, but I'm nervous. Bloody nervous."

"But no one knows about the shipments except you and me, Marty. How can he– "

"Because he's been on our bloody case. The man's a pain in the arse. He's got contacts across the water. Fleet Street. Who knows? Maybe he's been tipped off from Europe. I knew this was too good to be true. Fuck it, Lexy! I could almost smell the ink on the banknotes."

McGowan's fists tightened, the tattooist's ink spelling 'hate' gaining intensity as the skin on his fingers whitened under the pressure.

"What do you reckon, Lexy?"

"Don't know, Marty. Take him out?"

"You did deliver the note, didn't you? He did get it?"

"Yeah, of course– "

"Ger' on, Billy! Take 'em on son!" McGowan suddenly shouted, his concentration redirected to his son flying along the touchline, the ball at his feet, the game restarted. The boy's control of the ball showed a precocious confidence that enabled him to glide past the defenders in his path with ease whilst drawing others away from centre field, making space for his teammates to run into. He crossed the ball into the gap he had created in the defence and into the path of his centre forward. A tall gawky kid, the forward attempted to thump the ball goalward, but dragged it wide of the left post.

"Muppet!" McGowan groaned under his breath.

McGowan's presence on the touchline would not have gone unnoticed by the other parents. He had become something of a celebrity, and still recognisable in North Belfast even though he had moved out to the countryside. He was respected in his old neighbourhood. His reputation as a serial bruiser saw to that.

"Lexy."

"What, chief?"

"Jenkins."

"What about him, chief?"

"I think he might be heading for a car crash."

"A write-off?"

"We'll see. I'll leave that to you. I think you two need to have a little chat before we make any final decisions on that."

14

LOCAL MAN'S DEMO FOR PEACE...
Ballyblessington Spectator, May 1994.

*Ignatius Smyth, a tyre fitter from Fellrock, is doing more than
most to promote peace. Recently Mr Smyth started a one-man
protest on a traffic island on the Ballyblessington ring road. He
has been sitting on the same spot all day and every day ever
since. It is, he claims, a round-the-clock 'sit-in'.*

Dillon Jenkins, a spokesman for Mr Smyth, told the Spectator
*that the Fellrock man takes his demonstration very seriously
and doesn't know how long the sit-in will last:*

*"Iggy is protesting for peace. He was upset by the betting
shop shooting on the Antrim Road and wants to do something
to make a difference – to make people stop and think. His
protest is to underline the distaste that ordinary people feel for
the perpetrators of sectarian murder in Northern Ireland.*

*"Mr Smyth holds that now is the time for both communities
to stand together and show the terrorists that there is a popular
consensus for peace."*

*A spokesman for the RUC said that while the police have
every sympathy with Mr Smyth's views, they are responsible not
only for his safety, but also for ensuring the safety of passing
motorists and local residents. This is a major consideration
since Mr Smyth has chosen to site his protest at a road junction
on a busy dual carriageway.*

*"We have expressed our viewpoint to Mr Smyth on this
matter. We are, at present, maintaining a 'watching brief'. We*

are monitoring the situation, but will take immediate action should it prove necessary," the police spokesman explained.

On the Thursday morning, supplies of food started to arrive on the island. By lunchtime the trickle had become a flood. As with snow in spring, the deliveries were unexpected and unstoppable. Later, larger items were dropped off: a stove, a tent, a sleeping bag. The gifts – mostly second-hand garage junk – lay strewn across the island like the detritus of a shipwreck.

At lunchtime, plates of hot food came steaming across the surrounding tarmac borne by local residents, trailed by cats and dogs.

The catering was chaotic over the next while: some days meagre scraps and then on others overwhelming mounds of sandwiches and fast food takeaways – more than they could eat. Pungent hillocks of black bin bags, bulging with waste, sprang up and began to attract a diverse variety of wildlife to the roundabout. Organisation was required.

"Now do you see the power of the press?" Jenkins beamed triumphantly over a kebab. "This is the miracle of modern mass communication."

Smyth frowned.

By the end of week one, the chances of the two protesters surviving their barren environment had improved. They had shelter, they had food and they had bathroom facilities courtesy of the rugby club on the far side of the roundabout. Life on the island became sustainable, even tolerable. It seemed that the challenge would be less of a physical one and more to do with their ability to combat boredom. Jenkins mumbled about island fever.

They were buoyed however, by an awareness that their protest was gaining support. Dissenters, so far, were few. There was local dissatisfaction whenever the traffic paused to a crawl due to rubbernecking – then, and only occasionally, a voice might be heard shouting abuse from a passing car – but the disgruntled were easily outnumbered by those who tooted their horns or waved to give encouragement.

There might also be verbal abuse at the weekend from the odd binger staggering home from the pub. But the drunks were soon moved on or detained by the police, who were intent on containing the situation and putting a stop to any behaviour that would attract adverse publicity.

"Our first cloud," Smyth sighed.

"What?"

"This. It's our first cloud."

"What is?" Jenkins asked, sounding wary.

"The fuss."

"What about it? What's wrong?"

"It's too much."

"Oh, come on. One article in the *Spectator* is hardly 'fuss'. Anyway, it's just what we need, for God's sake. It isn't fuss, it's 'support'."

"It's not that that's wrong."

"Then what?" Jenkins sighed with impatience. But debating this – debating anything, for that matter – was better than the tedium of silence.

A frosty pause followed.

"THEN WHAT?"

"It's getting too easy," Smyth whispered, at last.

"What? The sit-in?"

"Look, I actually enjoyed myself yesterday."

"Good!"

"So tell me; what's that all about, Dillon? I mean, I'm not here to enjoy myself. I'm not here to have fun. I'm here to protest on behalf of a bunch of innocent guys shot in cold blood. I'm here for them. And yet here we are enjoying a celebrity picnic. Look, I'm here to focus attention on terrorism and human suffering, not to get my photo published in *Hello*."

"Now, that would be good coverage."

"You know what I mean, Jenkins!"

"Of course. But you're being too self-conscious. You don't have to play the martyr to get your message across. Anyway, you *are* getting your message across."

"What message? There is no bloody message."

"Well, mistake me if I'm wrong, but you told me you just wanted 'it' to stop. 'It' being the killing. 'Stop the killing'. That's a bloody good message. Nice and simple. You know, like 'Give peace a chance'. I can see it on a T-shirt."

"That's as may be, but I'm not the fifth Beatle, I don't give a damn about T-shirts and I'm not here to have fun."

"Look, Smyth, just because some misguided locals have nothing better to do than bring us the odd sandwich, doesn't mean to say we've gone soft. We're hardly living in the lap of luxury, are we? But we are ruffling a few feathers and we're getting noticed. And don't think for a minute the State is going to put up with our sideshow for too much longer. And anyway, do you really think the paramilitaries are going to let us share the headlines for long? I don't think so. This is just the bloody honeymoon, mate. As soon as you mention peace in Northern Ireland and start attracting support, you can be sure there'll be some hoodlums from one camp or the other waiting around the corner with a crate of petrol bombs and a box of matches at the ready."

"You don't understand me at all, do you?"

"Ok. Try me."

"Look Dillon, I agree with most of what you're saying. It's all pretty rational. Cause and effect. You do something and then people react to it. And then you react back, and so on. And so our profile grows. But you're seeing everything – this situation in particular – from their perspective."

"Err, who are *they*?"

"'They' being everybody. The people, the press, the police... society. You share their perspective. *You* share *their* perspective.

You know what to do, what to say, because you understand the rules of the game – what's happening now, what's going to happen next. You think like they do and they think like you. I don't want to think like you or them. I want to see beyond their perspective. Ok, so what *is* going to happen next? With luck the national press will pick up on our story, the TV news crews are going to arrive. Then if there's not much other news that week, we'll get our faces on telly for a while… blah, blah, bloody blah. It's all part of the same circus. But it's the same circus that killed those men in the bookies'. That is to say, the killing did the same for the UVF, UDA, IRA, INLA or whoever it was, as you expect this protest to do for us. That is, get us publicity. You see, it's the same endgame we're all playing, but it doesn't actually change anything. It doesn't lead to progress and never will. It'll neither unite Ireland nor secure our place in the UK. It won't end this bloody war."

"But it might help. It's a start."

"Yes, maybe it could. Maybe it is. But you're playing the same game by the same rules, with the same tactics. You're playing with people's lives. It's a game in which the rules never change and, meanwhile, a lot of innocent people die. As always, it's the least powerful and the poorest who are most affected."

"So what are you trying to do that's so different?"

"Suffer."

"How's that going to help anybody?"

"That's it, isn't it? I'm not sure. I don't know."

"I don't understand. I don't actually understand what you are saying or what you are trying to do here."

"Yes. Precisely. You don't understand. That's exactly what I am saying. It's not about understanding. It's about emotion, it's about raw bloody emotion. Raw and primeval and untapped and untamed. It doesn't matter if you understand, Dillon. This is about reacting. It's an agonised scream, it's wrenching your guts in public. It's not about making a sanitised, sensible statement. It's not rational. It doesn't work to a media plan. It's about getting angry, *being* angry. It's not about arguing or debating and reasoning, it's about being out of control and stamping your foot. It's about being unpredictable, insufferable and passionate and not being afraid to suffer. It's like self-immolation. It's an emotional response without concern for the outcome. The self-immolator doesn't know whether their demonstration is effective. They don't know the result. They just do it. They die. It's a sacrifice. It's martyrdom. Most of us are so wrapped up in our own well-being that we've lost the idea of sacrifice. Anything, any deed, any change of direction that might make paying the mortgage or rent any more difficult than it already is, is enough to paralyse the moral scruples of most. We've become a nation of slaves. We've become incapable of independent thought or action. We've become the marketing man's dream. They know us. They've made us greedy and they've got us tapped. They know where we live, what we do, what we want and what we'll buy. But there's more to life than that.

"Look, I don't understand what's going on here any more or less than you do, and that's just it. I don't want to understand. I just want to express my feelings in my own way. And I don't mind getting it wrong. I don't bloody care if we don't maximise on publicity. I don't care if we do or don't get any support. I don't care if we don't get our message across. I don't care if we're unpopular. I don't care if I die here of pneumonia. That – all of that – is my bloody right. And I am exercising it. I am simply pissed off about those eight men getting shot in the betting office and I'm reacting to it just however I feel like doing it. I'm simply expressing myself. Getting angry and letting people know. And I don't know if any of this is going to help or whether what I am doing is right. I am acting independently and doing it by my own rules. I've given up my job. I've left my home. There's no safety net for me any more and there's no going back. I haven't just stuck my head up above the parapet, I'm standing on the bloody thing and I'm waving my arms and dancing. And do you know something? So far it feels good. Damn good."

Smyth stopped; the wind blowing through the trees and the traffic's hum the only sounds to fill the silence that followed.

"Right, would you like a Penguin, Iggy? Go on. You can have it. It's the last one."

The idiocy stung.

"Do... you... hear... me... Jenkins?" Smyth asked in a deliberate and menacing tone.

"Of course I can bloody hear you!" Jenkins shouted. "Your voice is all I ever can hear!"

Suddenly they were interrupted by the appearance of a large be-suited man waddling towards them, mopping sweat from his brow with a handkerchief.

"Who the hell's this now?"

Anyone approaching the traffic island in suit and tie aroused suspicion. Those who came smartly dressed usually had something to sell.

"It's my editor. Look, I'll be back in a couple of minutes," Jenkins said quietly, scrambling to his feet. He straightened his tie, smoothed out his jacket, brushed down his trousers, tilted his head back, wrenched it from side to side till it clicked and then moved off towards the perspiring man. Jenkins walked slowly and with as straight a back as his heavy frame would allow. Decorum seemed important.

Dillon Jenkins' editor, Ted Montgomery, could put an arm around Jenkins' shoulder with ease. Jenkins was a large man, but Montgomery was a colossus. A touchy-feely type, he tried to enshroud Jenkins in the folds of his voluminous coat as they met in the middle of the roundabout. Montgomery wheeled him round as if they were chuck wagons expecting an Apache raid. They bowed their heads to conspire.

"What the hell are they talking about, Dog?"

Smyth patted the animal, then ran his fingers through the tuft of blonde hair that sprouted from the top of its head.

Dog and man watched the conference playing out before them on the roundabout. Smyth strained to interpret words, but could hear nothing. At times the protagonists moved apart and waved their arms expansively. At times they moved in close together when it seemed they were nearing agreement, but then there would be a breakdown and their expressions grew tense. There was animated body language, but nothing that could be translated.

The performance reminded Smyth of *The Old Man and the Sea*, as if Jenkins were the giant fish and his editor the old fisherman struggling to reel him in. Smyth could see that Jenkins was putting up a determined fight – thrashing his arms in resistance – and then weakening. The editor would move in closer and place a reassuring hand on Jenkins' shoulder as he sensed the moment of victory. But then breakdown; a twist and a turn away. Hands in the air and exasperation. It was a tight contest.

"What's he saying, boy?" Smyth asked, as he petted the dog.

Then it was over. The editor disengaged. He bustled back towards the spot where Smyth sat with the dog, and then on past, staring at the ground. There was a thunder in his expression that Smyth guessed the man would carry back to his office and unleash on a junior.

Jenkins wandered up to the traffic island bollard, dawdling in his editor's wake and at a safe distance. Smyth glanced into his eyes. He looked calm enough.

"What?"

"What 'what'?" Jenkins snapped back, growing stern.

"What did he say?"

"What do you think?"

"Haven't a clue."

"That's it," Jenkins said, loosening his tie.

"That's it, what?"

"He sacked me."

"Oh."

"'Oh' exactly."

"Welcome to the club."

"Don't be dumb, Smyth. This is important. I'm not about to self-immolate, like you. I truly am one of your selfish generation. And I've got a bloody mortgage to pay."

"But you're staying?"

"I want to see what bloody well's going to happen here, mate."

Jenkins removed his tie, bundled it up into a ball and tossed it over his head.

"Iggy?" Jenkins hissed after a lengthy pause – a silence that amplified the sound of their breathing.

"What?"

"Can you hear that?"

"What?"

"The absolute quiet."

"Yeah. So what?"

"The traffic."

"What about it?"

"There isn't any."

"Great."

"But there should be."

"Why?"

"Look, you big *eejit*, there hasn't been a bloody car come past for at least fifteen minutes, maybe more. Doesn't that seem a bit strange to you?"

They both looked up the dual carriageway, their eyes tracing the empty lanes.

A mile up the road, round the bend at the top of the hill, drivers stamped from brake to accelerator pedal and back as their cars crawled in the direction of Ballyblessington in a jerking conga chain. They were prevented from progressing further down the ring road towards the island by lines of cones and four traffic cops, arms swinging like pendulums, to divert traffic along the main road to the town centre. The policemen were not popular.

The view down the carriageway was one of abandonment and desolation: a surreal scene of a busy thoroughfare devoid of traffic, as though North Down had been struck by a deadly virus.

One cheek pressed to cold glass, DI Williams sat in the passenger seat of a patrol car – his deputy at the wheel. They were parked across the roundabout, a vantage point from where both the traffic and the ring road could easily be monitored.

"The cat's out of the bag now the press are here, I'm afraid, Murdoch," Williams sighed in a quiet voice with little emotion. "These two have led the horse to water and they've got it drinking away and quite happily, thank you. People'll be swarming here like flies on shite. All the cranks and the weirdos, the rent-a-mobs, the agitators and do-gooders. There's nothing like a demonstration for pulling a crowd. But why here? Why did they have to choose our little piece of hell?"

"What are we going to do, boss?"

"Not a lot. It's pretty much too late, already. Containment. We'll isolate them and hope it doesn't spread. But then, Murdoch – what the hell do I know?"

15

Thomas McShane's difficulties with sleeping intensified after the Antrim Road shooting. The gallery of ghosts had multiplied from seven to fifteen overnight. The ghost of Colin Downey seemed distressed – more so than usual – by the additional company; his one eye looked ever more accusing, his demeanour, meaner, the sense of Gothic grief deeper. McShane would never have believed that his insomnia could get worse, but it had.

The lack of sleep showed in his eyes. "You look tired, Tommy," had become his unwieldy handle.

Through the night the ghosts in the window came and went. Arriving *en masse*. Leaving *en masse*. McShane could cope with *them*, however. They were familiar. He could almost set his watch by their appearances. The apparition of Colin Downey was still deeply disturbing, still made him weep, but the others were welcome company for a lonely man.

It was the ghost of his marriage that really spooked him and kept him awake; that and the coldness of his rented bedsit – its drabness and the dilapidation. There was a carelessness reflected in the decor: the pink gloss paint and yellow wallpaper – the vilest pink, the sickliest yellow. An insult to eyesight. And whilst the paint was blistered and peeling, the paper curled away from the wall and flapped down towards his bed, threatening an avalanche of crumbling plaster. It made McShane's flesh creep.

And damp. Always the smell of damp. Musty and damp.

And his bed: a lumpy affair. A single bed, too mean for two, bullied the memory to be aware that he was on his own now. No body to cling to – to lie against for warmth. No breath to whisper to him through the night in reassuring snores: *I am here, I am here.*

The bedsit was in the middle of the maze of terraced streets that criss-crossed the Falls Road in West Belfast; an area that was beginning to be snapped up and patched up with yuppie money from Dublin and laundry money from Belfast – the keys then passed over to poor sods like McShane who could afford nothing better than to rent. And not by choice. He would rather be at home, but had been forced out. His wife was sick, he had been told. Suffering from stress. He must do the right thing, they said. Her family pressed him to go. Confused, he felt he had no option and surrendered to their pressure.

So he left, not wanting to make her condition worse. It didn't improve with his going. Her condition meant that she couldn't talk to him. Too stressful. Avoid all contact, she was advised.

He felt like a leper. What can you do when your very existence makes your partner ill? In the meantime another car had filled his parking spot. Another toothbrush had appeared in the bathroom holder.

She was burnt out. They both were, and now there was no one for company except the one-eyed ghost of Colin Downey.

McShane's departure from the marital home wasn't an ending, but a first step – the commencement of a trench warfare comprising explosive exchanges of solicitors' letters. Over the top. Grenades designed to maim, but not kill.

One letter that came during an early flurry suggested a figure for maintenance payments. It was so absurd it made him laugh. It became obvious that she would leave him penniless if she could have her way.

He planned to sue her now. Fight back. Take her to court. Adultery. Let the offices of state take charge. Ironic, he thought, that he would now be seeking help from the law profession, the senior members of which his people had been bumping off – or attempting to – for the last twenty-five years. Let them sort it out. Pity he didn't have a Gerrard Boyce amongst his legal team. In another life Boyce's iron will, attention to detail and killer instinct would have served him well as a barrister, he thought. And Boyce never lost an argument; a fearsome debater. Few who ever got close to winning an argument with Boyce lived to tell the tale.

Boyce! McShane hadn't seen him for days. Not since the Antrim Road shooting. Not surprising, since he hadn't given him the address of the bedsit. But Boyce would know where to find him. The whereabouts of anybody, anywhere in Belfast with a reputation such as McShane's were easily traced, spotted and reported back.

As soon as the high street was open for business at nine, McShane was out of his pit and in circulation. Some pampering was called for now. A bacon soda, a coffee, a paper and a trim.

"You look tired, Tommy."

"A number three please, Pat, and a shave."

McShane climbed aboard the blood-red throne and was cloaked from the neck down in nylon. The flimsy beige fabric made the hairs on the back of his neck tingle. Pat pumped the foot pedal at the base of the leatherette chair to tilt McShane back to an angle at which he could be snipped and snapped at with ease.

The barber revved up his clippers. McShane surveyed the room. The view brought a smile. *Thank God some things never change,* he thought, as he studied the black and white portraits displayed above the mirrors. The row of photographs featured clean-cut young men in their twenties, who – judging by their vintage hairstyles – would be nearing retirement age by now.

McShane wondered when a punter would have last challenged Pat to match one of the ancient hairdos on offer. Not for a while, if ever, he presumed. Most of the men modelled the hairstyles of the early seventies: trim, collar-length pageboy cuts, blown dry and teased to perfection – many set off by neat, topiaried beards and moustaches. There was an eclectic choice of mullet. The models, like a lost tribe of Noel Edmonds lookalikes, appeared sullen and serious.

"Coffee, Tommy?"

"Why not?" McShane replied, fearful of the insipid slop he was about to receive – coffee in name and colour only.

"Boyce was in here looking for you, Tom."

The combination of Boyce's name and a cut-throat travelling across his windpipe was unfortunate. McShane gulped, threatening a nick from the open blade.

"What did he want, Pat?"

"No idea. I'd rather you left me out of it, Tommy. He didn't say and I've no interest. I just wanted to let you know. Anyway, I said I hadn't seen you, and that's true. Now, don't go telling him anything different. Please Tommy!"

"Don't worry, Pat. Don't worry."

McShane shut up. He didn't feel like talking.

Clean-shaven, he walked back to his digs juggling a thousand worries, the trickiest of which being Boyce's interest in his whereabouts. Worrying about Boyce and the divorce at the same time was enough to make him want to flee the country. He'd love to go a long way away – as far away as possible, but knew he'd miss home as soon as he got there.

"Oi, Tommy! You can run, but you can't hide, son."

Boyce had slowed his Granada to walking pace.

"You look tired, Tommy."

"It's nice to know you care, Boyce!" *And no thanks to your slapping me round the face, you gorilla!* he thought.

"Want a word, Tommy. Get in!"

As McShane stopped, the nearside passenger door swung open. He felt deflated when he saw the young boy, Michael, sitting in the back. Michael flashed an evil smile to acknowledge him. The car sped off towards the M1.

"Do you want the good news, or the bad?" Boyce asked through a menacing grin.

"Bad," McShane said, abruptly. He couldn't bring himself to banter with Boyce and had guessed what was to follow.

"I've got a job for you. Right up your street. It's an in and out job. Nice and easy. Nice and clean."

"Great!" McShane said sarcastically, struggling to mask his lack of enthusiasm. "When?"

"In your own time. A week to ten days. I'll tip you the wink."

"And the good news?"

"After this one you're taking a sabbatical."

McShane could think of a pile of cynical retorts, but kept his lips buttoned. There was still a slight swelling and soreness from their last meeting.

"Oh, right. Thanks."

"Think of it as leave. We're not sure what to do with you. There are developments."

"What do you mean?"

"Well, there's talk of a ceasefire."

"Ceasefire? You joking? How come?"

"Where the hell have you been, McShane? You see, if you're not involved with the party, you won't know what the hell's going on. Look, you're not just fighting a war, McShane – you're also a part of a political struggle. And the political battles have only just begun, believe me."

They were already halfway down the motorway heading for Dungannon. Boyce handed McShane an A4 envelope. It was unsealed. When McShane slid a hand under the flap he was relieved when his fingers fumbled on only the one photo.

"I'll give you the where and when later," Boyce said in a detached manner. He turned the car off the motorway at Dungannon and looped over the carriageway to head back into Belfast.

16

Jenkins was beginning to find his nights on the island more tolerable. He had found the ground too hard at first and was continually disturbed by nocturnal din: car hum, mooing cattle and the scratchings from a nearby badger sett. There was also too much light: the constant yellow of the street lamps overhead and the luminescent amber of Belfast in the distance, which throbbed on the horizon with an H-bomb glow. At home he had always had difficulty sleeping with the curtains open.

By the second week however, he was starting to get the hang of things and adapting to living alfresco. Submerged in his polar sleeping bag and covered in a plastic sheet, in case of rain (and there had been none since the storm), he was warm and almost comfortable, and following the establishment of the police barricade, felt reasonably safe.

As the days passed the crowd of supporters grew – ever present during the daylight hours, then dispersing into the gloom as darkness fell. And as they retreated to the comfort of home, the daytime police were relieved by a night watch.

Rain came on the evening of day twelve. A lid of grey cloud had rolled across the sky and was followed by a steady drizzle. Jenkins and Smyth sat hunched in their sleeping bags watching from under a tarpaulin, which was propped up like an awning – their heads the tent poles.

"It's quiet– "

"Yes, so let's keep it that way. Look Jenkins, if you're going to start babbling, don't expect me to join in."

"Sure. No problem. I was just trying to convey the fact that it's quiet," Jenkins said, shrugging his shoulders, which made the rainwater run off the covering sheet in rivulets.

"Yes, I know it's quiet. I like it that way. It's not so quiet now, though, is it?"

"Right," Jenkins said firmly.

"Right."

"I'll keep quiet then."

"Good."

An awkward silence followed. The dripping of the rain seemed to increase in volume and exaggerate the tension.

"What!" Smyth suddenly shouted, his will snapping.

"Err, I didn't say anything."

"No, Dillon, but you were about to, weren't you. Weren't you! You're dying to. I can sense the desperation in your silence."

"Are you this wound up all the time, Smyth?"

"Of course I'm bloody not. It's you, man. Can't you see how irritating you are?"

"I'm just sitting here enjoying the view and keeping you company."

"Yes, but I know you want to talk... make idle chit-chat... have a natter... a chinwag, pass the time of day... well? Can't you get it into your thick skull... I don't?"

Another pause followed.

"Do you ever think about what would happen if God turned gravity off?"

"There you are, see? You just can't resist it, can you?"

Smyth thrust his head into his hands.

"It couldn't happen, anyway," Smyth mumbled after a tense couple of minutes.

"Why not?"

"Gravity is governed by the laws of physics. It's got bugger all to do with God."

"But if there is one, Iggy – a God that is – He'll be all-powerful. He'll have created the laws of physics and can fiddle about with them at will. Change them as much as He likes. Anyway, for argument's sake, say He switched it off."

"He can't."

"But if He did. Don't you wonder what would happen? Suddenly there's no gravity. We'd all just float off into space. The earth falling away from us below, drifting away... far, far away. And the first thing we'd notice would be how round the earth is. Round... perfectly round. A beautiful green and blue ball. And it would be like falling off a ball. We *would* be falling off a ball. It would be like doing a parachute jump in reverse. We'd drift away quite slowly. And then how long would it be before we'd suffocate? Not long; probably at fifteen to twenty thousand feet. Thing is, you imagine that buildings and trees would stick around at ground level behind us. Stuck there, slowly disappearing from view beneath us. But then of course that wouldn't happen, because they would fall off too. The topsoil, mud, clay – the whole lot would go... and the seas. We'd be the first to go, but we'd see all the stuff trailing after us... cows, sheep, lions and tigers... then a great mess of salt, sea and ice and mud and bricks. And then we'd pass out – suffocate as the air gets thinner and thinner. Or maybe sooner because of course, as we go the atmosphere will go too. In fact the atmosphere would go first, so we'd probably suffocate before we even left the ground... or... as we're just leaving it. We'd just have time to wave goodbye. Thirty seconds, maybe a couple of minutes at most. Two minutes of suffocation and the realisation that everything we've ever known is just getting sucked away. Makes you wonder though, doesn't it? If God was all-powerful and got really mad at us, He could do that. He could kill us all. Just like that, at the flick of a switch or in the blink of an eye. If He's got an eye."

Jenkins turned to look at Smyth, who sat stony-faced.

"What a load of shite."

"Makes you wonder though, doesn't it? Don't you have an imagination, Smyth?"

"Are you married, Jenkins?"

"What's that got to do– "

"Answer me. Are you married?"

"Err, no, actually. No."

"You were though, weren't you?"

"How the hell would you know?"

"I can tell by the hesitation in your voice."

"Well, what if I was?"

"What happened?"

"Don't ask."

"Well, if you like talking so much, then talk about something that's really important to you, like your marriage for instance. What happened there? What happened to your wife?"

"Maybe that's a difficult subject for me?"

"You said you wanted to talk."

"Yeah, but not about this. This is different."

"What? You mean you'd rather talk tittle-tattle – talk crap about God turning off gravity than talk about something that really matters?"

"No, not necessarily."

"Right then. So let's talk about 'you'. It'll be good for you. So go on then, tell me. Tell me what happened."

"What?"

"What happened to your wife?"

"Err, I don't know."

"Oh, come on, man!"

"I lost her."

"What, she's– "

"No, she's not dead. Nothing so final. She's alive and well and living in Chigwell. She left me. That's all. And it was probably my fault."

"You're divorced, then."

"Yeah."

"Don't tell me – you talked too much. Couldn't keep your mouth shut for a minute, I suppose."

"If you must know, it was my drinking. It got a bit out of hand. Well, completely out of hand. Well, I became dependent on it, to be honest. It helped me cope with the extraordinary, you see. You know, the awful news stories I had to cover and the pressure of work generally, but then it buggered up my ability to cope with the ordinary. Trouble is, see... I've got a large frame. A man my size can put a lot of the stuff away. A bottle of Scotch? No bother. I used to drink Scotch like it was tea. Got through cups and cups of the stuff. It helped me cope with what was happening at work, but then I couldn't cope with what was happening at home. I was constantly drunk. And then she couldn't cope either. Well, it's obvious really. And she wanted children. And in a way she had one... me. A bloody big kid. A horrible child: spoilt and demanding. But she wanted children and I couldn't oblige. Well, we could have got pregnant of course, but there was no way she would have had a child with me whilst I was drinking like that."

Jenkins sighed.

"I became a liability," he continued. "Then I lost my job. Staff jobs on the nationals aren't easily come by, you know. And once you get a reputation for drinking – for being unreliable – it's hard to get work. That's partly why I came to Belfast; to get sorted out. Well, the main reason, really. Get things going again."

"Do you really think Belfast's the right place to come to, to go on the wagon? You must be mad."

"Well no, but I was offered a job. Belfast is always newsworthy and I've been busy since I've been here. My contribution has been valued. Well, *was* valued. Looks like I've blown that now."

"Blown it?"

"Blown it."

"Yes, well. You'll not get back on your feet sitting around here with me."

"We'll see."

"And your wife? Any chance?"

"Remarried. Sad, really. Well, sad for me – I blew it."

"I'm sorry."

"No, I'm sorry. It was my fault. I just couldn't cope. I liked the idea of marriage. I embraced it. I married her, for God's sake, but then I couldn't cope with the reality. Frustrating really. I wanted it to work, *really* wanted it to work. And it did for a while, but I just couldn't see it through. It's tough because I don't know where to go from here. I guess wherever it is, I'll be on my own."

"You'll find someone. There's plenty more fish in the sea."

"Yes, but I don't like fish. Never have."

"You know what I mean."

"Yeah. Meeting someone else is always a possibility. But then what? I couldn't go through that trauma again. The break-up nearly killed me. I don't want to put anyone else through that, either."

"You're going to be a sad old man, if you're not careful."

"Thanks very much."

"Do you feel sorry for yourself?"

"Well, if I'm honest– "

"Be honest."

"Of course I bloody do."

"Ok. Let's move on. Maybe that's enough, for now. Anyway, do you feel better for that chat?"

"No I don't. No, not really," Jenkins sighed.

"Excellent! That just shows you then: too much talking doesn't do anybody any good."

"Don't you think it helps to talk through problems?"

Smyth locked onto Jenkins' eyes to cement his point with a cold stare.

"To my mind, you've only got one problem, Dillon. You talk too much, son. Far too much. Never underestimate the power of the quiet man. Be a quiet man."

Jenkins didn't answer.

They had heard the shouting, but took no notice; didn't interpret the commotion as cries of warning. Deep in conversation, Jenkins and Smyth had also failed to see the black saloon until it was nearly on them. It came rolling through the gloom, gathering speed, and silent. And it was that the large black Citroën was getting faster, but without the engine revving – the whistling quiet – that fired a rush of adrenaline when they realised that it was freewheeling towards them.

When the car failed to take the bend on the final approach to the roundabout and began to career like a bobsleigh against the crash barrier on the central reservation – and as it clipped the kerb, flipped up and started to barrel roll gracefully through the air – they still expected it to stop somehow or brake or just slow and follow the curve of the road around the roundabout.

But still the car came crashing on. Then the tinkling of glass shattering, followed by a high-pitched screeching as the vehicle hit the pavement on its side. They could feel the friction in the soles of their shoes as the car juddered across the stone slabs towards them, spraying plumes of bright orange sparks.

As they looked up they were frozen in the car's headlamps, which illuminated their island as if it were a stage and their stunned faces the masks of Greek tragedy.

In the final seconds both men tried to fling themselves clear, but were restricted by the sleeping bags still wrapped round their legs. They could do no more than tumble sideways like fallers in a sack race. And just as the car slewed across the island it started to lose momentum, grinding into the concrete before coming to a standstill; its front end looming over the traffic bollard – coming to rest at a forty-five degree angle, the nearside wheel thrust into the air and still spinning with the rusty scratching sound of a stuck record.

Then hissing and smoke.

"Bloody hell, that was close! You ok?" Jenkins shouted to Smyth as he staggered to his feet.

There came no reply.

17

"Smyth! Smyth! Where the hell are you? Smyth!"

Jenkins' yells reverberated through the dark cloud which had enveloped the island. He coughed; choking on the cocktail of burning engine oil, exhaust fumes and dust.

Through the smoke Jenkins spotted Smyth's sleeping bag and could see the outline of Smyth's legs. He was lying beneath the front bumper of the car. The Citroën was tilting across the bollard at a crazy angle, propped up at the front and looking as if it could crush him at any time.

Jenkins froze for a moment, his brain struggling to make sense of the mayhem. The moment seemed an hour, until Jenkins heard an explosive '*pumph*' and saw flames dancing out from under the car's bonnet; a stream of burning fuel rolling across the island from the driver's side. He grabbed Smyth's sleeping bag and pulled hard, hoping that Smyth would come with it. With a sharp tug Jenkins shifted the bag, and though it was sodden with rainwater it came away easily in his grip. But Smyth was left behind, his legs exposed and lying in a puddle of watery fuel – his overalls darkening from navy to black as they became waterlogged.

"Smyth, Smyth!" Jenkins shouted again in desperation, then driving his shoulder into the nearside front wheel, raised high in the air and still spinning. He hit the car with force. A large and heavy man, he managed to barge it back and slide it off and away from the bollard. He looked down, could see that Smyth was free of the wreckage and grabbed him with both hands to pull him clear by his overalls. Jenkins leaned back, dead-lifted

Smyth off the ground and then staggered away from the burning wreckage, tottering in zombie-like steps towards the safety of the roundabout.

With his back to the Citroën and having deposited Smyth on the grass, Jenkins was about to turn to run back to look for the car's driver, but froze when he was suddenly illuminated by a brilliant flash of yellow – flinching when the car's petrol tank exploded.

Jenkins sank to one knee and shielded his face from the heat and bright light with his arm.

"Oh, God! The driver!" he whispered.

"There wasn't one," Smyth croaked.

"What do you mean?"

"There wasn't a bloody driver. I could see. Must have jumped clear."

"You sure? Are you absolutely sure?"

"I looked. I could see!"

"Ok, ok. Are you all right?"

"I don't know. My head's very sore," Smyth mumbled in a hoarse voice, then coughing on fumes and phlegm.

"Shall I contact Peggy?"

"No, no need. Look, I'm fine. Don't fuss. She'd only bring us more of her bloody sandwiches. They're her answer to everything."

"Are you sure now?"

"Don't fuss. Please, don't fuss... aagh!"

Smyth winced as he tried to sit up.

"You ok? I think we should get you checked out."

"Look, Jenkins, I don't want any bother."

"Always the bloody martyr!"

Soon the emergency services arrived. And as men and women in luminous jackets tackled the car wreck, the flames of the inferno flickered and hissed, while the flashing lights of the fire tender and ambulance created the ambience of a macabre disco. A body bag and a shovel were produced. Neither was required.

A paramedic directed a torchlight into Ignatius Smyth's red-ringed eyes.

"Follow my finger. What's your name?"

"Smyth. Ignatius Smyth."

"What day is it?"

"Haven't a clue."

"Ok. Mmm, maybe a slight concussion. You'll live. But we'll need to get you examined properly to be sure you haven't got a fracture."

Smyth was lifted onto a trolley-stretcher, strapped in and wheeled off to the ambulance which was straddling the empty lanes of the roundabout. With Smyth stowed on board the first paramedic swung the rear door of the ambulance shut as a second ushered Jenkins into the back. Soon the ambulance was accelerating up the dual carriageway and heading for Belfast.

Jenkins, sitting in a fold-down seat at the rear of the ambulance, watched as the emergency workers busied themselves at the accident scene, lit by the dying flames of the fire; the glow dying quickly under clouds of foam. And as the workers shrank from view Jenkins turned away from the rear doors to check on Smyth who was propped up on the trolley which had been clamped to the side of the ambulance. Smyth looked groggy and barely conscious.

The two paramedics were squashed in side by side and facing Smyth. They were both clad in green overalls and yellow safety jackets. Both wore boots, caked in mud. Now that the ambulance was underway they had pretty much left Smyth to himself. Jenkins thought their lack of interest at odds with good bedside manner.

And there were two of them in the back with a third at the wheel. This struck Jenkins as strange. He thought ambulance crews came in twos, not threes. He looked over at the driver. He was wearing black jeans and a black nylon bomber jacket. No uniform. Odder still.

Strange, Jenkins thought. *And how inattentive these two paramedics are.*

Since the ambulance had driven off, neither of them had laid a hand on Smyth; no checks, no tests. They hadn't even taken his blood pressure. And they hadn't offered him any reassurance or asked him any of the diagnostic questions normally expected. They just sat poker-faced and nervous; quiet, disinterested... negligent even. They merely stared through the front windscreen at the road ahead.

Then Jenkins noticed their hands. They were bare. They weren't wearing gloves. *Where were their latex gloves?* Since the spread of AIDS and the HIV virus he assumed paramedics wore them as a matter of course, like condoms for the fingers. And their hands were tattooed. When he noticed the tattoos, a dark thought came to him, and it was as he was deciphering the legends of the North Belfast division of the UDC that Dillon Jenkins glanced over at the ambulanceman nearest to him. The ambulanceman looked down to his hands, splaying out the fingers and inspecting the dark blue and red scrawl dyed into the skin, looked up at Jenkins, smiled and then curled his fingers into fists as he rose to his feet.

"I think this guy likes my tattoos, Lexy," the man said, with a hint of irony, before making a sudden lunge. Jenkins felt a cracking pain across the top of his head, and then the world turned black. Lights out.

For the crew of ambulance E92, the night had had its excitements. Braced for the normal routine of sweeping up young bingers from the pavements of Belfast and taxiing them to the nearest Accident and Emergency Department to have the booze pumped out again, the evening had proved more eventful than usual.

An ectopic pregnancy at around eight o'clock had required an urgent pick-up and high speed drive across the Craigantlet Hills to the maternity wing of the Ulster Hospital; and later, at about ten, a cardiac arrest in Belmont Drive, East Belfast, had required immediate resuscitation – heart massage and mouth-to-mouth – before a dash to the Royal Victoria. But these were nothing compared to the drama of the emergency call-out to the Fellrock roundabout on the Ballyblessington ring road which followed.

It had sounded like a straightforward assignment over the radio. A car crash. Get there fast and attend to any casualties as necessary. All routine. But then they were flagged down on a quiet country road *en route*, ordered out of the ambulance at gunpoint, stripped of their uniforms and forced to jump, semi-naked, into a roadside ditch.

Freezing cold, wet and muddy, they emerged to see their vehicle being driven off into the distance by their assailants: three burly men in balaclavas who even had the cheek to switch on the siren as they went.

18

"Sit them there. Not there! There! *There* on the sacking. On the bloody sacking!"

When he regained consciousness Jenkins found he was being pinned against a door, but couldn't see by whom from under the hood that had been pulled over his head. It was a coarse fabric that scratched and smelled of potatoes. Then he heard the thud of someone being thumped, then a moan.

He imagined he was being held by one of the phoney paramedics, possibly the one who had coshed him – the big guy. Whoever it was, was gripping his shirt front and holding him upright by jamming him against the door frame with both hands.

Jenkins looked up, squinting through the loose weave of the sack into the gloomy light of what he took to be a barn.

"Hey! watch the fists!" he heard Smyth grunt through a gag hanging half-off. He too was being grappled with by one of the paramedics who had him locked in a 'full nelson' – arms bent behind his back with the ambulanceman's bulbous biceps and forearms interlocked with Smyth's and forcing his head down onto his chest.

"On the bloody sacking, I said. ON THE BLOODY SACKING!" the main man shouted again. The nervousness in the voice worried Jenkins, as though the man were trying to psych himself up to be brutal.

Jenkins was bundled down onto something with the height and width of a sofa, but firmer and offering more resistance. His head was jerked back as his hood was yanked off. He could see nothing in the dull light that gave a clue to their location, but the smell was agricultural. The middle-of-bloody-nowhere came to mind. The barn was about the size of a double garage. Tools, saddlery and DIY clutter were scattered around machinery draped in tarpaulins and sheets. The floor was of dried mud covered with clumps of straw.

Jenkins looked to his right to confirm that the body which had landed in beside him was Smyth's. It was. But for the gaffer tape, which had been reapplied, Jenkins imagined that Smyth would be complaining by now.

Thank God for gaffer tape, he thought.

The biggest of the men approached Jenkins and ripped the gag from his mouth, taking a layer of skin from his top lip with it. Jenkins could taste blood.

"God! That hurt– "

"Shut him up, Johnny," the main man, Lexy Danvers, ordered.

Jenkins got a thump in the mouth. Then the bottom lip didn't feel too healthy either. Tenderised, they were a matching pair.

"Ok, ok. There's no need– "

Another slap. It caught Jenkins across the right cheekbone. It stung more than it hurt.

"Ok, Johnny. That'll do for now. There's no need to go overboard just yet. I want their attention and I think we're nearly there now, aren't we, gents?"

Jenkins and Smyth risked a brief nod. Jenkins wondered why Smyth's gag hadn't been removed too. And even though he enjoyed the peace and quiet, the panic in Smyth's eyes – which were dancing like bingo balls – was infectious.

"I hope you enjoyed our runaway car. Dramatic, huh? That was Billy, there. A fine performance. Billy rarely misses a target. Very good ten-pin bowler, Billy. Now, gentlemen... you're probably wondering why you're here."

"Well, I guess it's so we can join the 'disappeared'."

"The 'disappeared'? I think you've got your sides mixed up,

Mr Jenkins. It is Mr Jenkins isn't it? Dillon Jenkins?"

"God! You know my name."

"Naturally."

"Well?"

"You're English, aren't you?"

"Welsh."

"All the same, you've definitely got us confused with the other side. And I thought journalists were supposed to be knowledgeable."

"You're not republicans then, I take it?"

"Very funny, Mr Jenkins," Lexy Danvers chuckled, his laughter quickly echoed by the sidekicks.

"So what the hell are we here for?"

Danvers nodded over to the big one, Johnny, who stepped forward and slapped Jenkins across the face again.

"We're asking the questions, Mr Jenkins."

"Oh, like the Gestapo?"

"Yes, you've got the picture. And like them–"

"Yeah, I know... *Vee haff vays of making you talk.* Look, talking's my forte. What can I tell you?"

Another nod from Danvers, and another slap swung in.

Jenkins winced, his head already sore from the coshing in the ambulance. The pain reminded him of a migraine he'd once had – a one-off induced by paint fumes inhaled when decorating a mate's bedsit – so severe he'd thrown up.

The slaps weren't too painful, but the sudden jolts that accompanied them exacerbated the effects of his headache: a splitting pain that shot down through his right eye to linger in the roots of his teeth.

"You know why you're here, don't you, Jenkins?"

"Actually, no. I don't know why I'm here. And I'm amazed you know my name. It's got nothing to do with unpaid parking fines has it, by any chance? If so, I'm very sorry. I know I've picked up quite a few of them recently. Belfast City Council haven't put the collection out to tender, have they?"

Another slap. Another wince and more shooting pain.

"Not funny, Mr Jenkins. And this isn't the time to be funny, either. See your friend there. He's going to die if you get this wrong. And so are you."

"Can I have a clue, then?"

"Are you pissing about, Jenkins? 'Cos if you are son, your teeth are going to be poking out of your arse very shortly."

"No. Seriously, what do you want to know?"

"It's what *you* know, Mr Jenkins. We want to know what *you* know."

"Why? I really know very little."

"You're an investigative journalist!" Danvers screamed, whilst signalling for another slap. This time, as the back of the large guy's hand swung across Jenkins' face, one of his fingernails caught Jenkins' lip creating a small tear. The blood dripped freely. A familiar taste, now.

"You're a journalist, Jenkins. A fucking investigative reporter. You're paid to find out stuff about people like us. But it seems you've found out too much, I'm afraid. And I want to know how much, who you've told and what they're going to do with what you've told them."

"Hang on. McGowan. This is about McGowan, isn't it?"
Silence.

"It is, isn't it? It's about McGowan and his drugs. Oh for God's sake, man – everybody knows about that."

"What do you know about 'that'?"

"Nothing that isn't common knowledge already. Nothing that anybody's going to print anyway. If you really want to know, I took a story to my editor, but he wouldn't touch it."

"I've got bad news for you. I don't bloody believe you!"

Danvers was losing patience. His eyes were staring madly. Jenkins didn't like the look. The eyes lacked warmth – were black, impenetrable and inhumane. Danvers began prowling about the barn, with an excitement and excess of energy that Jenkins felt sure was going to be unleashed on either himself or

Ignatius Smyth. Then Danvers punched his hand into one of the main roof supports, a fierce blow after which he kept his hand pressed into the wooden column. He looked up into the roof beams and screwed his fist into the post, his eyes closing and the smallest of smiles escaping across his lips. It was an expression that hinted at a lust for pain. Danvers looked down at his fist, the knuckles grazed and oozing blood. Suddenly he swung round and slapped his open hand hard across Jenkins' face, smearing blood over his victim's cheek; he leaned down to Jenkins' ear and whispered:

"I don't want to hurt you, but I'm going to have to kill you, if you don't co-operate. Do you understand? Do you *fucking* understand?"

Danvers grabbed Jenkins by the hair and jolted his head back, so that Jenkins had trouble focusing on him as he strained his eyes to see. He tried to move his head, but Danvers' grip was too tight.

"*Yeeers,*" he croaked.

As Danvers let him go, Jenkins rocked forward and sprawled on the floor beside the bales of hay he had been perched on. He would have wiped his face, but his hands were still tied.

Danvers spat on the floor beside Jenkins, beckoned to his cohorts and stepped out of the barn.

Jenkins rolled up onto his backside, leaned back against the bales and looked over to Smyth, who could do no more than wiggle his eyebrows.

God knows what that's supposed to mean, Jenkins thought.

The barn was quiet now, except for the hiss from a gas lamp hanging overhead. It seemed more unnerving with Danvers gone. The anticipation of what he might do when he came back, to whom and with what implement, was worse than the reality of his kicks and punches.

About an hour later, Lexy Danvers returned, followed by the two characters who'd played the roles of ambulancemen. They were struggling into the barn with another hooded victim who

– judging from their mumblings – was also gagged, and – judging by their clothes and shape – was female.

"Simple question. Simple answer, Mr Jenkins. If you know so little, why didn't you print the story we planted?"

"What story?"

"You know."

"Look, I'm not trying to be funny, but what story did you plant?"

"Look, Jenkins, see this?" Danvers said, whisking off the woman's hood. "You might not care about your health or that of your friend here, but I doubt if you would want to see anything happen to her."

Danvers had revealed an angry and confused face; the terror in her eyes exaggerated by her gag.

"Oh my, God! Peggy– "

Jenkins received another slap; almost a punch. He struggled to stay conscious.

"No! Please. Just tell me. Please, give me a clue. What story did you plant?"

"The one I stuck through your door, you pillock."

"Office or house?"

"Don't be smart."

"Office or fucking house?"

Jenkins' patience was also wearing thin.

"Your fucking house!"

"Look, seriously – I haven't received anything. Anything! I'd remember. I haven't received anything out of the blue, special or different, for months and months. Please, please believe me!"

Danvers grasped Peggy Smyth by her left wrist. Shaking his head in disbelief, he whipped her arm until she was bent double over the large trunk beside the main column of the barn.

"Don't make me do this. Don't make me do this, Jenkins," Danvers growled, his teeth gritted. Peggy was staring at Jenkins, her eyes pleading for him to help – Jenkins panicking to remember something, anything that Danvers might want to hear.

"I just don't– "

"DON'T MAKE ME DO THIS!"

Danvers twisted Peggy Smyth's hand down onto the top of the trunk and forced the fingers open until they were splayed out flat. He produced a six-inch blade with ugly serrations.

Jenkins gasped at the terror in Peggy Smyth's face.

"See this?" Danvers said with menace, whilst raising the knife high over his head in his free hand. "See those?" he continued, nodding down towards Peggy's fingers. "I expect you're a bit peckish by now, Mr Jenkins, aren't you? How do you fancy some finger food?"

Peggy was staring wide-eyed, mumbling muffled shouts and shaking her head as much as the pressure Danvers was exerting on her arm would allow. Danvers lowered the knife so that the teeth of its serrated edge rested on the little finger of her left hand.

"It's not so bad. I guess she's not going to miss these. She's right-handed. I noticed when she tried to slap me earlier. But then the longer we're here, the more fingers she's going to lose and the fuller your stomach's going to get. Only five fingers to go before we start on her good hand."

Danvers pressed the knife tight to Peggy Smyth's finger. It drew blood in a small spurt. Peggy Smyth's wide-eyed stare got wider.

"Don't. Please don't hurt her. For God's sake! I really haven't got a clue what you want!"

But then, out of desperation, Jenkins remembered the strange mailing with the large sheet of paper and the cut-up letters.

"Hang on, you can't be talking about the envelope I received last week? Ah, I get it now. That crappy piece of paper and the letters... you need a pot of stronger glue, mate. Is that what this is all about? You're going to kill us over a soggy piece of paper and a bag full of sodding letters? Your note was totally illegible.

Couldn't read it. Made no sense. Bloody hell! Have you got problems, mate."

Danvers released the pressure on Peggy Smyth's finger and looked up at his men, scanning their faces to see how alert they were to this possible blunder. Their expressions were blank. They weren't great listeners at the best of times.

This reassured Danvers, who stayed stern-faced, but knew he'd probably cocked up and dreaded the thought that McGowan might find out. He would ensure that he didn't.

Peggy Smyth sunk to the floor, cradling her bloodied finger in her good hand. Both she and Ignatius Smyth were mumbling through their gags. It surprised Jenkins how the sound of panic can be deciphered even in a mumble. He couldn't hear exactly what they were saying, but thought they might be reciting the rosary.

"For fuck's sake, shut them up!" Danvers screamed, disturbed by his sudden lack of ideas and direction, and disoriented by the realisation of his mistake.

Stunned by their leader's fury and violence, the henchmen froze. Danvers took it upon himself to deliver the pain. He left Peggy Smyth slumped over the trunk, so as to step over and kick Smyth in the stomach and Jenkins in the ribs. Both were winded. Both gasped for breath.

"For God's sake, man. What? What can I do? What do you want to know?" Jenkins wheezed.

"Don't you see, you imbecile? It's too late for you. It's too late now. It's too bloody late!"

Danvers had Jenkins by the hair again and was pulling his head back and staring into his eyes from point-blank range.

"Look, whatever story you tried to plant, I didn't get it, all right? All I know is that McGowan has started dealing in drugs, that's all. I wanted to do a story on it. It was going to be pretty general... the paper wouldn't let me name names. Anyway, they wouldn't touch the story with a bargepole. Look, I'm a journalist. I'm only doing my job, for God's sake. I'm sure the bloody police know about your operation. Special Branch must do!"

"As I say, I'm afraid it's too late, Mr Jenkins. I don't give a shit about all that. It's just too late. It's just too late for you now. You're *here* and you're *here with me*. You know too much and have seen too many faces. I'm sorry."

Jenkins didn't like the defeatism in Danvers' voice. He prepared himself for another blow, if not the *coup de grâce* – a bullet or something – but Danvers stuck another strip of gaffer tape over Jenkins' mouth, bound Peggy's hands and swept out of the room indicating for his men to follow. The barn fell silent again save for the hissing of the gas lamp and the muted sobs of Peggy Smyth.

Jenkins lay still, numb and with neither the energy nor courage to move.

Oh, so he needs permission before he can kill us. How pathetic! Jenkins thought.

Unable to free his hands or feet, Jenkins laid his head on the bale nearest to him, exhausted.

Danvers didn't return that night. The anticipation that he might at any moment made for a torturous ordeal for his captives. Jenkins imagined he was arguing their fate in a kangaroo court somewhere. That Danvers might kill them on his return was a possibility that kept them all awake and staring at the wooden sides of the barn until the gas lamp ran out of fuel. Then they waited in the dark for dawn and for the sound of Danvers' footsteps as he came back to finish the job.

19

Jenkins stared up into the eaves of the barn for inspiration. His eyes, fingers and toes were the only parts of him that he could move.

"Hey, God! Remember me? It's your son, Dillon Jenkins. Why hast thou forsaken me?"

Jenkins never prayed.

"Because you're a waste of space, Dillon. You've squandered every opportunity I've ever given you. I gave you a talent—"

"What for?"

"For writing, you eejit. And what have you done with it?"

"Fair enough. Not a lot. But what about Smyth and his sister? What have they done to deserve this? I know he can be hard work, but he's trying to do something useful, now—"

"What? Sitting about on his arse, Dillon?"

"Yes, very funny God, but you get the picture. And what about his sister. What's she ever done to harm you?"

"She stole a tin of sardines from the Donaghadee Co-Op in 1984. I saw her do it. She might have been short of a bob or two, but still – that's no excuse for criminal behaviour. And she never asked for my forgiveness afterwards, you know."

"Don't be so picky, God. You know what I mean."

Dillon Jenkins had always imagined God in the guise of the traditional icon: a large man in white flowing robes with white hair, white beard and a booming voice. The God Jenkins could see now was less conventional. He wore a red robe with white fur trim. It didn't take long to make the connection. God the Father... Father Christmas. *That's it!* Jenkins realised. *They're one and the same. God is Santa! It's so obvious! How fantastic!*

And God was talking:

"I'm afraid I can't help you, Dillon. It says so in the rules. Divine intervention and all that. It's not allowed. Direct action would impinge upon your freedom as a man to choose for yourself."

"But I'm not going to be a man for much longer at this rate. Anyway, what about miracles? You've parted the Red Sea, can't you strike these people down with something that will incapacitate them for a while whilst we run away? I mean, you don't have to kill them. A small dose of plague would do, or a sudden bout of 'flu."

"Dillon, Dillon. I've never performed a miracle in my life. The Red Sea and the rest, they're just wonderful coincidences that man has assigned to me. Sorry, Dillon. Anyway, as I say... rules is rules."

"You wrote the bloody rule book. Can't you change it?"

"That's cheating, Dillon. I'm God. I can't cheat. If the Supreme Being were to cheat, where would that leave us?"

Jenkins gave up on prayer. It was the kind of half-hearted effort that only the most desperate of atheists would attempt as a final throw of the dice. He hoped he might be offered a cigarette and a last meal. Sod the steak and chips, he'd ask for something hard to source like a leopard burger or dodo pie or maybe suggest a visit to an all-you-can-eat salad bar.

A patch of congealed blood at the side of Jenkins' mouth was irritating the skin and making it itch. He couldn't reach it with his hand or tongue. He thought it strange that it was this minor ailment that was so bothering him now rather than the grim fate that awaited him at the hands of Danvers.

He would have contemplated an escape from the barn, but couldn't shift or loosen the ropes burning into his wrists and ankles. Exhaustion and hypothermia had sapped his stamina and persuaded him that it was easier to give up and hope for a miracle. The least he could do and did, however, was to wriggle over to Ignatius Smyth and his sister where they were huddling together, as best they could, for added warmth. Jenkins lay on his side, wedged in between them like a log in a woodpile. He rubbed his mouth against Smyth's shoulder which brought instant relief from the itching.

Jenkins tried, but couldn't sleep. He distracted himself with a rewind through his life and career. He gave up after a review of his 'A'-Level results. How *had* he only scraped two 'E's? It was all too depressing and only added to the stress. Too nervous. All night. A long night. Too alert, waiting for footsteps that wouldn't come. He dreaded the sound of the footsteps. He dreaded too, the first sign of the daylight that would bring them. But slowly, slowly, dawn came, leaking the new day into the barn through the narrow cracks in the wooden planking. Then he heard footsteps. They were coming back. His throat, dry and thirsty, brought a lump hard to swallow.

Jenkins looked at the other two. They were also awake and returned startled expressions. A wink was the best offering of reassurance that Jenkins could articulate. Each of them then rolled into a seated position. They listened and watched for clues, their senses sharpened, as chains were manipulated and bolts drawn back.

Shortly the rattling stopped. With tense muscles and clenched fists, they waited for Danvers and his two sidekicks to appear in the doorway. Jenkins saw that tears had begun to roll down Peggy Smyth's cheeks. He thought he could hear whimpering. Smyth's eyes, too, were moist. Jenkins tried to make his gaffer tape smile, but to no effect.

Dawn. Sunshine burst into the barn drenching the captives in yellowy light as the double doors were folded back. The interior was now exposed like the open front of a doll's house; the sun dazzling them and preventing them from identifying the approaching figure whom they could only see in silhouette; the dark silhouette of a short stout man.

"Jesus, Mary and Joseph!" the shadowy figure muttered.

The stout man scampered over to them and set to freeing the hands of the first bundle of humanity he came to.

"Thank yo– "

"Shh!" the dark figure interrupted, putting a finger to Peggy Smyth's lips and looking fierce.

As Jenkins' eyesight adjusted to the light he could see that the man was middle-aged and, judging by the trembling in his fingers as they fumbled with the ropes, terrified. He wore the tweeds of a country man and a battered felt hat.

Once freed, the man allowed them a few seconds to stretch, then ushered them out of the barn by waving his arms to compel them to hurry and also to keep quiet.

As they ran into the field they were dwarfed by the landscape; the hills of South Down undulating towards the Mourne Mountains and, in the foreground, a spectacular view of Strangford Lough.

"What's your name?"

The man shook his head and waved a finger to hush them again before driving them like sheep down across the grass towards the lough shore. Once they had struggled over the dry stone wall that bordered the field at the bottom, he indicated for them to follow the footpath heading south along the lough.

"You're on the Ulster Way here. Keep following the shore for about three miles. That way, it will bring you into Killyleagh. You'll be ok there, and please, you haven't seen me, all right? Please forget you ever saw me. I could lose more than just my job for this."

"Thank– "

"Shh! Not a word now!" the man cautioned before turning his back on them and scurrying up the field as fast as his stocky legs would allow. He stopped once, however, to look over his shoulder to make sure the three were moving away, and then continued back to the barn in a hurry to shut it up. He must leave it as he had found it – exactly as he had found it. Hugh

Campbell would postpone the cutting of Mr McGowan's lawn for yet another day.

The three ragged figures shuffled on along the shore path in silence, too intent on survival to make any unnecessary sound. They hurried, limping and staggering, only slowing to help one another where the path narrowed, was rocky or obstructed by gorse. Smyth held a hand to his brow, his head still sore from the concussion.

They didn't think or care to look back and therefore failed to see the bigger landscape upon which Hugh Campbell stumbled towards the barn, and missed the drama of Campbell being encircled and then swallowed up by a cordon of RUC men – swooping down towards him in a long line across the hill.

Interspersed between policemen in flak jackets, brandishing handguns and automatic weapons, were dog handlers struggling to rein in their Alsatians; the dogs slobbering and yelping in excitement at the chase. As they closed in on him, Campbell fell into the long grass, curled himself into a ball and braced himself for a beating. He only looked up when a hand came to rest on his shoulder.

"It's ok, Mr Campbell, you can get up now. It's ok; you've got nothing to worry about, man. We know who you are. You can get up now."

As he got to his feet Campbell caught sight of two groups of policemen – one taking potshots at Danvers whilst chasing him across the field, the other grappling with his two accomplices up beside the house. He watched as the men were handcuffed and forced into the back of a police Land Rover.

Along the shore the escapees turned a bend in the footpath which took them around a large rock. On the far side they hobbled into a detachment of four policemen, whose dog startled them with its barking. Jenkins blew out his cheeks as the nearest officer moved forward and offered him his arm to lean on. Peggy Smyth sank to the ground, smiling through tears of relief.

20

Thomas McShane hadn't seen his wife for at least two weeks. Not since he'd moved out of the house. He hadn't missed her much. Not surprising when he considered the bickering and long sulks he had had to endure before packing his bags. They hadn't had an adult conversation for months. She had had nothing to say to him whenever he phoned to enquire about his mail, the household bills or any of the other domestic trivia.

When he stopped to think about her and evaluate his feelings, usually whilst lying in bed at night staring at the ceiling, he decided that he didn't miss her in an everyday sense, but missed the way they had once been. It was a memory distorted by nostalgia – nostalgia for the days when they had been a 'real' couple; the days when he considered that they'd been happy – the first five or six years. Life had seemed simple then. They had been very close; inseparable. That was before '81. Before the hunger strikes. Maybe that's when the cracks had begun to appear; when he had got suckered into the troubles, had gone out on the streets, had learned to mix a Molotov.

McShane sieved through the memories to find the truth of how she had been with him before those times – how she had treated him then. Did she ever respect him? Was he more forgiving then? It was confusing, but he knew he should feel guiltier than he did for his part in their failure.

He was careful to guard against nostalgia, warning himself that there was no going back. His wife didn't want to anyway. She'd moved on, had found someone else and now he wanted that too. He didn't want to dwell. He wanted to be positive and give himself a second chance.

Then, quite out of the blue, he bumped into her on the Falls Road. He saw her coming from way in the distance, at first just a blur. But it was her. He knew.

He didn't think she'd seen him. Not at first, anyway. But then, as they neared each other, she couldn't help but see him and couldn't avoid walking past him. She was on her own and as unprepared as he. She neared. He looked up. She looked down.

"Hiyer!" he said and offered a smile. She ignored him and walked on in silence, head bowed.

Not even a 'hello'! he thought. *God, she must be mad at me.*

Nothing had prepared him for the disappointment he felt, and it surprised him. It wasn't as if he wanted her back. Things had been too rotten, for too long. So why?

Frustration. It must be frustration. The frustration of knowing that she still loved him (why else would she bother being mad at him?), knowing that in some way he still loved her and that there was nothing that either of them could do about it. People love whiskey, he thought, but too much whiskey is poison; just one bottle can kill. Sometimes you have to give up the things you love most.

He had to give her up. He just wished she could be civil, but knew she couldn't be and knew it was foolish to expect it. At least they had something left – still shared something intimate: hostility. Hostility bred of a fear of each other and of a fear of going back, only contradicted by the memory of what they once had and had been together. Tragic that it was past, though. Tragic that they hadn't learnt to harness the passion and use it for their mutual benefit.

McShane walked on and was heading down to the Grosvenor Road roundabout on his way into town when Boyce came by in his Granada.

"Hey, McShane!"

Boyce pulled up beside the footpath and kept pace with him.

McShane looked up and met Boyce's intimidating stare with

a blank expression. Boyce's bullying had no effect on him now.

"Hey, McShane! Don't forget our little job, will you? Time's moving on."

McShane had been expecting that Boyce would be growing impatient for him to act on the latest brown envelope. Oh, well. So be it. And anyway, if what Boyce had told him about a ceasefire was true – and the word on the street appeared to confirm it – then this really could be his last assignment.

"Where're you going, McShane? Want a lift?"

McShane shook his head and walked on. He wouldn't flatter Gerrard Boyce with either conversation or company.

"Weirdo!" Boyce mumbled under his breath before accelerating away with a screech of tyres.

McShane was relieved. His prospects were improving. Get the next hit over with and then get the hell out of Northern Ireland. It sickened him to have to perform another kill, but – as had become his way – he would be detached and try not to care. Shoot or be shot had become his fate, but now that way of life was coming to an end. There was hope for him and maybe even a future.

A future? Maybe he should emigrate to Australia or New Zealand. Somewhere far away where he was unknown and could make a fresh start. A fresh start in a young country with well-balanced people. Bliss! He'd go somewhere where no one cared about religion and tribal differences. And, God! how exciting it would be to meet someone new – to fall in love again.

McShane wondered if he had the mental strength to overcome his past. Had he been scarred by his history? Would his ghosts travel with him? Would he be haunted for life? Surely the ghost of Colin Downey wouldn't be there? Maybe he'd have to give religion another shot. Perhaps God could help him. But then, you can't *make* yourself believe in God.

He shook his head and increased his walking pace, keen to get to Kelly's Bar for a stiffener. Time was of the essence.

21

A sudden shower threatened the four schoolkids who were making their way to the bus stop at the bottom of the Upper Newtownards Road in East Belfast. They were relieved to reach the protection of the bus shelter before the shower intensified and to be saved from a soaking. The journey to school in the city centre was grim enough on a dry day.

They were less than pleased then, when the next passing car, a dark blue Vauxhall Astra, clipped the puddle beside their stop and doused them in a thick wave of dirty rainwater; their white socks turning grey and their flannels saturated for the day.

Much jigging about and shaking of legs followed and an exchange of knowing looks. Unmarked police cars were easily enough recognised in Belfast. Blue or red Fords or Vauxhalls. No dealership sticker or vinyl in the rear window. No tow bar. Sometimes two rearview mirrors. Often tinted windows.

The navy Vauxhall racing up the Upper Newtownards Road was heading for North Down. Headlights were on full beam. The rush hour past, the morning traffic was flowing freely. Its two passengers stared out from their back seats into the gloom, their identity concealed by the smoked glass. The car was past the schoolboys in a flash. Their plight went unnoticed.

The policeman driving flicked on BBC Radio Ulster to catch the news:

"Early yesterday morning RUC Special Branch officers secured the release of two men and a woman who were being

held against their will in a barn near Killyleagh. Officers freed the captives in a dawn raid. The abducted men, who have been named as Ignatius Smyth and Dillon Jenkins, were taken into protective custody and have since been assisting the police with their enquiries.

At a briefing this morning the RUC press office issued the following statement:

'On Wednesday night a vehicle was rammed into a roundabout on the Ballyblessington ring road endangering the lives of two peace protesters – Mr Ignatius Smyth and Mr Dillon Jenkins. Mr Smyth was injured during the incident and an ambulance was called. On its way to the scene the ambulance was hijacked by an armed gang who then used it to abduct both men and transport them to an isolated barn near Killyleagh. Later that evening, members of the same gang seized Mr Smyth's sister from her home in Fellrock.

'Yesterday morning the three kidnap victims were freed by officers of the RUC's Special Branch in a raid at first light.

'During the police operation a large quantity of crack cocaine was recovered with an estimated street value of three million pounds.

'A group of men suspected of being members of the banned Ulster Defence Corps are to be charged later today with a variety of offences related to these incidents.'

Newstime spoke to a solicitor representing the two kidnapped men, who denied that his clients had accompanied the police willingly:

'The police have an issue with my clients' peace campaign and have used this incident as a pretext to detain Mr Smyth and Mr Jenkins in order to intimidate them. The police are suggesting that the men's peaceful activity is a threat to public safety. The men refute this. Furthermore, we are of the opinion that the police's handling of my clients' protest to date can best be described as "incompetent".

'Smyth and Jenkins are innocent men and must be allowed

to continue their peace campaign without any further interference.'

...Reports are coming in that the car bomb left outside a petrol forecourt in Newry last night could have–"

The driver switched off the radio.

"Shit! What did he have to say all that for?" Ignatius Smyth moaned from the back seat. Jenkins said nothing, but glanced up at the front mirror to check the police driver's reaction to the story. Their eyes met briefly before the driver looked away. Jenkins kept staring at the mirror to see if the driver would make eye contact again. He didn't.

Dillon Jenkins folded away his copy of the *Telegraph* and turned to look at Smyth. The unmarked police car was heading for Smyth's house in Fellrock. They were travelling well over the speed limit judging by the pace of other cars, which seemed to be progressing at a crawl.

"Who?" Jenkins asked, after a long pause.

"*Who?*"

"Yes. Who?"

"Who, what?"

"Who had to say what for?"

"Oh, Craddick. Craddick, the solicitor... about the police and our 'campaign'."

"Where did you find him?"

"Craddick? Oh, he kind of adopted Peggy and me a while back. He acted for Peggy when she had some serious bother a few years ago."

"Oh?"

"Don't ask. Anyway, I'm sick of people talking about 'a campaign'."

"Look, Smyth, you big *eejit*, it's about time you faced facts. This *is* a campaign. Ok? It's a bloody campaign! If it wasn't before, it is now. Why do you think we're attracting so much attention from the press? No one minds a protest – they're pretty benign – over and done with quickly. But a campaign can spread like a cancer. And this is... has. It's too late, man. You've cracked it. You're front page news."

Jenkins waved the front page of his *Telegraph* under Smyth's nose. The headline was stark:

BELFAST BUSINESSMAN IN DRUGS BUST.

"Actually," Jenkins continued, "why *was* your Mr Craddick so aggressive? You'd think he was trying to start trouble, not stop it. That's the last thing we need. They won't let us sit on the island now, you know. Not the police. Not now. You've got too many people's backs up."

"That's a bit rich, Jenkins."

"What?"

"Well, you say that I've got too many people's backs up, but *you* nearly got us killed back there. Really nearly killed, but for the grace of God. I mean, why the hell did you want to go stirring up a hornet's nest like McGowan's for?"

"I'm a bloody investigative reporter. What do you expect? It's what I do. I had no choice. Look, it's all very well sitting on an effing roundabout feeling sorry for yourself and whingeing about this atrocity or that, but I do something that actually makes a difference. And, in this instance... it has!"

Jenkins dumped his newspaper on Smyth's lap and pointed to the headline to prove his point.

Smyth turned away to look out of the window.

"I suppose you must be gutted you missed your scoop. Funny you've ended up *in* the story," Smyth said quietly and without turning back.

They sat awkwardly for a mile or two.

"How's your head, Dillon?"

"Bloody sore!"

The men had been released from Castlereagh RUC station on the stroke of eleven. Cars carrying photographers and reporters had followed them as they were driven away; darting about behind them in desperation to snatch a photo.

The police driver carpeted the accelerator the moment they hit the Castlereagh Road and lost the pursuing pack. There were three or four pressmen waiting for them when they arrived at the Smyth residence in Fellrock, however.

"For God's sake, they're like rats. You get rid of one or two, and then another half dozen pop up in their place," Smyth groaned.

"Hey, I'm one of– "

"Well, they say you're never more than eight feet away from a rat."

"Oh, thanks very much."

"Don't take it personally," Smyth mumbled.

Jenkins clambered out of the car and headed up the garden path.

"Good to be home, eh?"

But Smyth was off.

"Where the hell are you going?" Jenkins called, turning round to see him striding away from the cottage in the direction of the ring road. "Are you not going to drop in? Not even for a minute? *No, obviously not,*" Jenkins murmured, rolling his eyes. He broke into something like a jog – more of a jiggle – to catch up with Smyth.

"What about Peggy?"

"Peggy'll be fine. She doesn't like fuss. She certainly won't like the press hanging around."

The press were, indeed, drawn away from the house as they followed Jenkins and Smyth.

"*News Letter*, Mr Smyth. Are you going to continue your protest?"

"*Mirror*, Mr Smyth. Do you have anything to say about the kidnapping?"

Smyth ignored the pressmen who scuttled along beside them like crabs. He also ignored the cameramen who kept one step ahead, hopping backwards whilst snapping and then spinning round to gain more distance before repeating the performance.

They might as well be invisible for all he cares, Jenkins thought.

And Smyth was giving a masterclass in self-control; calm in the face of flashgun fire.

Jenkins struggled to keep up.

"*Ballyblessington Spectator*, Brendan Tulley. What did the police ask you, Dillon? Will they let you go back to the island?"

Dillon Jenkins stopped for Tulley. He knew he should make an exception for the local man. He greeted Tulley warmly and gave him enough words for a quote.

Jenkins would have loved to engage with the reporters. He knew what they wanted and what would make them go away, but *he* wasn't setting the agenda and wouldn't break Smyth's code of silence. As he was approached by the reporters, Jenkins waved them away as if swatting flies.

"No comment!" his hands shouted.

It took a hundred yards of pushing and shoving before the pack of newshounds gave up, turned and trotted back to their cars before speeding past to ambush Smyth and Jenkins at the roundabout.

"You know, if you'd just give them a quote or two they'd stop bothering you."

"Really," Smyth replied, yawning.

"Look, they just need something to write, man. They've got to write *something*, so you might as well give them a few lines that they can repeat word for word. It doesn't even have to be the truth. Just don't give them an excuse to be inventive."

"Is that how it's played?"

"Yes. And you're right. It's a game. So you might as well learn the rules– "

"Rules?"

"Yeah, rules."

"You, have rules?"

"Better believe it. And you've got nothing to lose by playing along."

"Do you expect me to?"

"No– "

"Good. Well, for once you are perfectly correct, Mr Jenkins."

"But you know you're going to have to put up with a lot of this crap from now on. And what's more, if you're not going to play along, you'd better not be hiding too many skeletons. They can detect even the slightest whiff of a scandal from miles away."

They walked on in silence. Cars passed. Some honked their horns. A couple of kids trailed them on motor scooters whilst overhead a police helicopter whirred; a distant speck. They strode on at a brisk pace ignoring the commotion as best they could, still too drained from the kidnapping to make any real sense of the situation. Smyth was more concerned for the safety of the kids on scooters who had to weave across the road to round the large number of parked cars.

"We could have stopped off at your place to check on Peggy... had a shave... grabbed something to eat," Jenkins whinged.

"There's time enough."

"What are you going to do when you get back to the island, anyway?"

"You know," Smyth replied in his understated monotone.

"Look, there's a good chance that they won't let you back. They don't want you to carry on. You realise that, don't you?"

"Maybe. But, you never know."

Jenkins stopped and took a firm grip on Smyth's sleeve to prevent him from progressing further.

"*What?*" Smyth asked, testily.

Jenkins stared into his eyes, his grip tightening.

"Just wait a moment, Smyth. We need to talk. Things really are getting out of hand here."

"Tell me about it."

"Seriously! Things have changed."

"Yes. And for the worse, since you turned up."

"Look, they might have arrested one bunch of thugs, but there'll be others. The reality is that you're in danger now and what's more, you know it."

"Damn right. And I put that down to you and your bloody journalism."

"Oh, come on!"

"Oh come on, what?"

"Look, I can't help that McGowan twigged that I was doing a story."

"No?"

"No, of course not. Anyway that's history, let's concentrate on what we're doing here and now. Look, catch yourself on! How the hell can you go back to sitting on that bloody traffic island after what you've just been through? Can't you see the kind of people you're dealing with here? Can't you see how effing exposed you are? The police don't want you there. The paramilitaries don't want you there. I don't want you there. Nobody wants you there– "

"You've made that quite clear from day one."

"Ok, maybe I didn't really understand what you were doing then. No, not at first, but then I did. Well, up until those thugs intervened. And now? Oh, I don't know. Things are different now. It's too bloody dangerous. Whether you intended it or not, and whether you like it or not, yours will now be seen as a political agenda. You're making headlines. You must know that there are people here who aren't going to like that. None of them like sharing the front page. You've stuck your neck out and now people recognise your face. You're becoming a target and it won't be rotten eggs they'll be throwing at you. There are forces at large that you're not equipped to handle. Look. Seriously. It's time to go home."

"Well you know that's not going to happen."

"Ok, ok. But listen, they're going to be coming after you and they know where to find you now. Well, that's if the police let you back onto the island in the first place. Look, you'll be a sitting duck there! Literally, a sitting duck." Jenkins paused – could see his words were wasted. "Well, I guess if you are going back, Smyth... and, well, obviously you are... the good news is that as long as you're attracting publicity, the police will be there in numbers. You'll at least get *some* level of protection. And whilst you're newsworthy – for a short while, that is – the press will be around. But once they tire of you and they've moved on, then you'll be vulnerable. You know – not now, but later."

"Have you finished?"

"Yes I have. But I'm just warning you to be careful."

"Got a conscience?"

"No, not yet."

"Fine. Anyway, what about you? What are you going to do? Are you coming back with me or buggering off?"

"Coming back."

"Right then! Let's stop wasting time, shall we?"

Smyth shrugged himself free of Jenkins' grip and continued walking. Jenkins looked up. The island wasn't far. He could see the tops of the trees bordering the rugby ground on the far side of the roundabout and the thick crop of satellite dishes which had sprouted like fungi above the media motorhomes parked in the neighbouring field.

At street level, a large mob obscured their view of the road junction itself. The volume of the crowd's din increased as they neared – disturbing and incomprehensible.

Smyth and Jenkins reached the outer ring of onlookers and started to squeeze their way through. They recognised many faces along the way and found they knew a few by name.

A cheer went up; the crowd parting as they progressed. Many leaned forward to offer words of encouragement or to pat Smyth on the back. Jenkins grinned proudly as he followed Smyth into the throng of waving hands.

Soon they reached the police cordon and Detective Inspector

Williams, who stood in their way, his manner detached and stern. The cheering crowd and the swooshing of the surveillance helicopter, plus the antics of the media, were a challenge to the RUC officer's calm demeanour.

"What do we do?" Jenkins hissed at Smyth.

"We keep going."

Smyth caught the inspector's attention and walked directly towards him.

My God! He's smiling, Jenkins realised when he caught a glimpse of Smyth's profile as he turned to greet the crowd.

As Smyth finally emerged, the crowd hushed, enthralled. Cameras continued to flash, the helicopter whirred high overhead, but otherwise, silence.

Smyth kept moving towards the inspector, his smile now widening into a grin, and brimming with confidence. As Smyth closed on him, the inspector's expression changed from cold indifference to confused consternation. Just as Smyth reached him, the inspector seemed to dither, and then at the last moment, shot out a hand, which Smyth grasped and shook heartily before patting the man on the shoulder. Smyth leaned over and whispered something, inaudible above the noise of the helicopter.

Whether it was Smyth's words or just his friendly demeanour, whether the detective inspector was acting on orders or was just determined to keep the peace in a volatile situation, DI Williams stood aside and allowed the two men through. The cheering erupted again, accompanied by a volley of camera flashes, as they walked across the junction towards the island.

The island! The debris had been swept away by the road services and the broken pop art bollard replaced. A ghostly imprint of the runaway car had been scorched into the tarmac.

The two plonked themselves down in their usual places at the foot of the bollard and resumed their vigil. A swarm of newsmen and women buzzed about them shouting questions. A couple of policemen moved forward and reined the reporters in, shepherding them back behind the crash barriers recently placed at the side of the road. Onlookers gazed on with the gormless expressions of visitors to a zoo.

The buzzing of the crowd paused again when a radio was heard from a parked car, crackling with the lunchtime news:

"It is reported that Mr Smyth and Mr Jenkins, the 'Fellrock Two', have returned to continue their sit-down protest on the Ballyblessington ring road..."

The crowd applauded, till someone called for quiet.

"...When questioned, a spokesman for the RUC said: 'There is no question of the Royal Ulster Constabulary making a U-turn on this matter. We want the two protesters to find a safer site for their campaign. Our prime concern has been, is and will be, one of public safety. Following recent incidents we are also concerned for the safety of Mr Smyth and Mr Jenkins. Officers have secured the immediate area and allowed the men to return on a temporary basis until a more suitable site is found.

'Whilst the RUC are happy to acknowledge the validity of the men's peace protest, it should be understood that we are also mandated with the maintenance of public order. It is vital that the province's roads and highways are kept open and free from obstruction. At present, local and commercial traffic is being redirected away from the area, along the old Ballyblessington to Belfast road. This is only a temporary measure however, whilst we negotiate with Mr Smyth and Mr Jenkins. The situation is subject to continual review.'

A solicitor, who claims to represent the campaigners, was reported as saying that the RUC's prompt action in allowing the men to return to their island has helped ease tension and is a positive and constructive development. The solicitor added, however, that the RUC's suggestion that this was a temporary measure did not bode well for future co-operation. He added that he could well remember the police doing little to keep roads open during other political protests in Northern Ireland."

"He's sacked!" Smyth said, abruptly.

"Who? Craddick?"

"Craddick. Bloody hell, Dillon, where did all these people come from?"

Leaning back against the bollard, Smyth surveyed the crowds with a mixture of pride and bewilderment. Proud of their newsworthiness, but bewildered by their loss of privacy. The sea of dancing eyes stunned them both into silence. Neither noticed the dog lie down on the pavement beside them, exhausted by the heat.

22

Spring had moved into summer. Days of sweltering sunshine and constant bickering.

"So why *did* you do it, Ignatius?"

"Do what?"

"This."

"This, what?"

"This protest."

"What about it?"

"Why did you start it?"

"It's a bit bloody late to be asking me that now, isn't it? Anyway Dillon, you *know* the answer."

"Yeah, the Antrim Road thing. Well?"

"Well, that's why."

"Yeah, but why *that* one– "

"That one, what?"

"Why that particular shooting? There's been so many. So why that one? And why now? Why not last year or the year before? There's got to be another reason. People don't just drop everything just because they've been upset by something they've heard on the news."

"Don't they?"

"I don't think so. Well, not ordinary people like you and me; people with businesses and mortgages. Sure, you get the odd Bob Geldof/Mother Teresa type – but why you?"

"I'll tell you what, son. Why don't you just invent a story for me? I bet you have a talent for that kind of thing."

"What? Because I'm a journalist, you mean? Pah! Oh, but hang on though, I can tell that there's something more. There is a reason you're here. There is, isn't there? Your reticence is a bit of a giveaway... *and you look guilty,*" Jenkins whispered, leaning over and searching Smyth's eyes for clues. Smyth turned his face into the breeze.

A period of chaos had followed their return to the island. Unfortunately for Ignatius Smyth's modest aspirations, his sit-down protest had caught the public imagination and become the flavour of the month with the UK tabloids. It was also now regularly featured on the television news. The men's sacrifice had an immediate appeal with the public – a refreshing antidote to the 'me-ism' that marked the years of the Conservative government.

To a Northern Ireland riven with conflict, the sit-down protest offered a fresh alternative to the warped motivation of the warring factions and their dedication to violence. The simplicity of the gesture and the modesty of the setting had a pathos that illuminated the tragic brutality of the troubles and communicated a simple message that crossed cultural borders. The image of the two men sitting by the bollard became familiar, their notoriety quickly spreading – reaching an ever wider audience – reaching Europe, attracting the attention of, and drawing comment from, any and all of those political leaders with a need to shore up their vote by aligning themselves with 'just' and 'popular' causes.

TV crews descended on the roundabout, comprising nationalities from further and further afield. Questions flew across the police crash barriers like arrows at Agincourt, posed by the ranks of reporters desperate for a quote. Every flinch, shuffle or facial expression triggered a salvo of flash photography, the media circus fully aware of the public's appetite for a freak show.

That the Fellrock Two were attaining celebrity status came as anathema to Smyth. But the mixture of sacrifice and anarchy that their protest engendered – the challenge to authority and the hardships they endured – encouraged debate at all levels in society. Dinner party chit-chat, drink-addled pub talk and radio phone-in programmes explored the motivation of the protagonists and the efficacy of the protest. It was discussed in bus queues, canteens and common rooms.

"It was an escape," Smyth said to Jenkins, turning back out of the breeze and speaking slowly.

"What was?" Jenkins asked, struggling to conceal his surprise that Smyth might be about to reveal something of himself.

"This, the protest. I thought I was going to suffocate before. It was like living in a prison cell."

"What was?"

"Life. Before this, before the sit-down."

"Oh."

"I wasn't very happy... wasn't really enjoying life... hated the routine. I couldn't cope. The pace. The responsibilities. The bills. The finance. The relationships– "

"What relationships? You haven't got one."

"Exactly. Work. Ambition. Religion. People. Northern Ireland. The Troubles. Family. Friends. Guilt. Catholic guilt. Christmas cards– "

"Christmas cards?"

"Oh, you know. Not sending them... not getting them... forgetting them. You know... the guilt of letting people down."

"You've got to be kidding. Is your life *that* complex?"

"Everybody's life is *that* complex. Everybody's kaleidoscope is confused. With every twist the beads form more and more complex patterns. Abstract patterns that are hard to read and make less and less sense... too much detail... too much bloody detail! You know, the endless lists of stuff to remember: get the windows cleaned, fix the guttering, get the boiler serviced, the car MOT'd, tax the car, insure the car, insure the house, remortgage the house, sell the house, clean the house... it just goes on and on and on... I feel like a time traveller sometimes. You see, my heart is that of a farm labourer dodging typhoid and consumption in the late 1700s, enjoying the great outdoors, but then my head tells me that I'm a working man in the 1990s struggling to repay a mortgage, keep a car on the road and pay about ten types of tax – and all on a pitiful wage with few benefits and no holidays. Meanwhile there's a technological revolution going on all around me that I can't keep up with and which makes me feel a fool. Actually we're all travelling through time. We've all been travelling through time together – through the fifties, the sixties, the seventies. We're all travelling at the same pace though, which is why we never really notice. We all have the same velocity. Well, all except for the Teds that is– "

"Teds?"

"Teddy boys."

"Oh?"

"Stuck in a fifties' time warp."

"Oh, right."

"Yeah, but we're mostly time travelling together. It's a bit of a one-way street. Always heading into the future. No one's worked out where the reverse gear is yet. I mean, how to travel backwards. Well, I've found the handbrake; I've pulled it on damn hard and jumped out of the time machine. I might have lost all my material possessions, but I've gained all the time in the world," Smyth said with a grin, not much more than a tic. It cheered Jenkins to see Smyth's face animate into a positive expression. A milestone. He took it as a sign of confidence; an intimacy.

"What about your job? Was it really that bad, Smyth?"

"It was killing me. Slowly killing me. Monday to Friday was always horrendous. A horrible routine. I felt like I'd been institutionalised – probably was. I'd crawl through the week struggling to Wednesday, and then, the sense of relief that the week was half through and the weekend looming was just too ridiculous. The weekends were ok, like being let out of prison on home visits for good behaviour – release on parole. But if you wish away your weeks you can end up wishing away months, years, and I'm not up for that. There's more to– "

"Isn't it like that for most people, though? Isn't that just the working life? I mean, we've all got to work, Smyth."

"Do we?"

"Depends on what you want out of life."

"Not a lot actually. Materialism just maintains the slave state. Supports the status quo. Keeps us in our place. Keeps us in our place of work. I mean, if religion is the opium of the people, then materialism is the crack cocaine. There's not much that I find attractive about the twentieth century, actually."

"So what era do you hail from?"

"I don't know. I just know my spirit comes from the past and that I have difficulty coping with the present. I wish I could go back fifteen or twenty years. It's still only about 1970 in my head."

"Sure, Smyth. I think Slade must have been moon-stomping across your brain cells and done some damage. The seventies were pretty crap too, especially here."

The men paused for breath. It was early morning and already Ignatius Smyth had conjured up an exhausted silence.

Then there came a loud rumbling; the noise of approaching traffic. Somewhere in the distance a backfire highlighted the drone of diesel engines. A long weaving line of vehicles soon came crawling down the carriageway from the direction of Belfast, dilapidated and choking. It was still only about seven – an hour before the commuter rush beyond the barricades. Jenkins and Smyth were standing, trying to wake up and get their blood circulating, surveying the scene and sipping tea.

A caravan of trucks, vans and camper vans appeared through a fog of grey fumes. Smyth and Jenkins looked up, looked at

150

one another and then over to the dual carriageway where the advance party was descending towards them, anointing the air with burning oil fumes. The men's expressions reflected their surprise that the police had allowed the column access to the ring road.

The decrepit vehicles snaked into the rugby club car park on the far side of the roundabout, pulled up and began unloading.

A human chain spread from the car park out across the carriageway and onto the roundabout. Boxes and bags, bed-rolls and kitbags were passed from hand to hand, person to person, then received and distributed by a dedicated team who dashed about pitching tents, stowing kit and lighting fires to establish a base camp on the grass.

The motorised vanguard was soon joined by reinforcements on foot. Finally, a delegation approached the traffic island; a bedraggled group of three: a tall one, a short one and a fat one – all of indeterminate gender and all dressed in the turn of the century uniform of black leggings, Doc Martens, knotted hair, nose piercings and loose-knit sweaters in garish colour combinations.

"Mr Smyth?" the lead boy, ginger-haired and gangly, asked in a West Country accent and looking towards Jenkins.

"He's Smyth. And who are we?" Jenkins asked, abruptly.

"We were at a jazz festival in Cork and heard about what you're up to here. We thought you might like us to join your peace camp. We read about your protest and we'd like to play a part."

"Where?"

"Here?"

"No. Where did you read about it?" Jenkins asked.

"The papers."

"Which?

"Err... the *Sun*, I think."

"What are you doing reading the *Sun*? You look more like

Guardian readers to me. Well, if not the *Guardian*, then at least the *Independent*."

"We like to keep an eye on what the right wing are saying and doing," a second boy – the short one with glasses – interjected in Estuary English.

"Yeah, right!" Jenkins said scornfully.

"Look, everybody is welcome here," Smyth interrupted. "All I would ask is that you treat this place with respect and do nothing to antagonise the police or local community. Oh, and by the way, our protest isn't political, it's humanitarian. It's a sit-down demonstration for peace to honour the eight innocent men who were shot by terrorists in Belfast earlier this year."

Jenkins was impressed with Smyth's short speech. He hadn't heard him deliver a soundbite to the public before and was startled by his composure. Neither had he heard Smyth attempt to define their mission. Until now, Smyth had always been enigmatic – enigmatic but vague, and yet here he was presenting the definitive story.

"Yeah. That's cool. We know the score. We're like foot soldiers, but, kind of laid-back foot soldiers... not like shock-troops. Nothing nasty," the ginger-haired one said brightly.

"Yeah, peace-loving foot soldiers. Like a Quaker army, a battalion of pacifists. You know, like... first out of the trenches and first over the top, but offering the peace sign," the be-spectacled one added.

"And then they blow you away," Jenkins said cynically under his breath. "Anyway, sounds like you're perfect for us. What do you reckon, Smyth?"

"God help us! Another bloody army of Brits trying to sort out our problems," Smyth sighed.

To conclude the meeting, the third one, a girl – a shy and quiet girl – presented the brown parcel she was hiding behind her back to Smyth.

"What's this?" Smyth asked trying to sound friendly.

"Open it," the girl said in a soft, barely audible voice.

Smyth opened the package with trepidation and care, trying not to tear the brown postal paper or to appear too eager. He anticipated that it would be some despicable piece of craftwork: maybe a model of a dove fashioned in lentils or a fertility symbol woven from cat hair. He was pleased when his fingers found fabric, soft and cool to the touch. Smyth slid the cloth from the envelope. It was a length of turquoise silk, flecked with gold.

"What is it?" Smyth asked politely.

"Not 'it'... 'they'," the ginger one corrected.

"They were given to us by the Dalai Lama. We met him last month. There's two – one each. They'll bring you good karma," the bespectacled, serious one said.

"They might help keep you warm at night," the quiet girl added, coyly.

"Why, thank you," Jenkins said, moved by the gesture.

The delegation returned to the roundabout and continued with the work of lashing ropes to timber, banging large pegs into the ground and unrolling lengths of canvas.

Smyth and Jenkins retired to the island to observe the comings and goings of their guests from their bollard. Peggy Smyth was waiting for them.

"Now look what you've done," she tutted.

"What?"

"These people – who are all these people?"

"Reinforcements," Jenkins said undaunted.

"They seem a nice bunch," Smyth added with enthusiasm.

"Have you two gone quite mad?" Peggy Smyth said boldly.

"Wha– "

"Do you think that people round here are going to put up with this? I'd look after your own first, if I were you. I mean, what if these people upset the police? This place is going to become a magnet for any fringe lunatic with a cause. Can't you see that? Haven't you had enough trouble?"

An awkward pause followed.

"Did you bring us anything to eat, Peggy?" Smyth asked coyly.

"Yes. Two rounds of sausage sandwiches."

"Oh, thank the Lord!" Smyth said, frowning at Jenkins.

"You've the brain of half a rocking horse, Smyth," she mumbled at her brother, her attention suddenly caught by the large banner – a painted bedsheet stretched between two poles supported by guy ropes – being hauled up on the edge of the roundabout and facing the ring road: 'SMASH THE FASCIST STATE'.

"See what I mean?" Peggy Smyth said, turning back towards Fellrock.

23

Peggy visited the island most days. It had been a good summer to be out of doors. However, she never stayed overnight, always returning home in the twilight. She felt a bond had developed between the three of them since their ordeal in the barn, and was keen to be in their company.

The kidnapping had been an extreme experience, but strangely intimate, something others couldn't share or understand. The three didn't discuss it. Didn't feel the need, and bristled when others brought it up. With time, she felt sure, the memory would dim, but the bond would always remain strong.

"It's nice to see you so calm and relaxed, Peggy," Jenkins told her, the next time she dropped by.

"Yeah, we're a hardy bunch," Ignatius Smyth said, butting in as he wandered over.

Jenkins glared back to encourage him to give them a wide berth. Smyth shrugged and sloped off in the direction of the latrines which had arrived earlier that week courtesy of the local council. They were a Mecca for flies.

Once Smyth was out of earshot, Peggy grasped Jenkins by the arm and leaned forward.

"Do you like my brother, Dillon?" she whispered into his ear.

"That is a complex question. Do I like him? God, I've never really thought about it."

He didn't welcome the question, but he liked that she was leaning in close to him.

"Of course you have."

"Like him? Really *like* him? I don't actually know. I think of our relationship as being a professional one. It's like we've started a business and are colleagues."

"I don't think he'd like to hear that," Peggy said, leaning back and sitting up straight. Jenkins was disappointed, missed the intimacy of feeling her breath on his ear.

"Really? Why? Do you think he cares? I don't think he gives a toss what any of us thinks. He's one of the most single-minded individuals I've ever met. You've got to admire him for that. Quite old-fashioned, but admirable. I mean, he's on a mission. Well, more a crusade really. And actually, when you think about it, his way of looking at the world *is* mediaeval. He thinks I'm a heretic. He'd burn me at the stake tomorrow if it were still legal."

"I thought *he* was supposed to be the Joan of Arc in all this?"

"I think he's more of a Robinson Crusoe, Peggy. He's living on a desert island, after all. And, I guess, I'm pretty much his Man Friday. We do seem to have a master and servant thing going on. I think he assumes he can civilise me."

"Ok. Interesting. But answer my question: do you like him?"

"Of course I like him. But then I don't really know him." Jenkins paused and drew on his cigarette. "Anyway, what does it matter what I think? Why do you ask?"

"Because I don't really know him either. I'm his sister and I don't know him very well at all. He doesn't make it easy, you know?"

"Yeah, I can see that."

"Underneath that gruff exterior, he's quite straightforward really. You get what you see with him. He just shies away from intimacy, that's all. Oh, I don't know. Anyway, what about you, Dillon? What are you like?"

"Complex."

"Nice complex, or nasty complex?"

"A bit of both. Depends on my mood, I suppose."

"And are you going to let him down, Dillon?"

"What do you mean?"

"Are you going to let him down – betray him? He trusts you, you know."

"The thought had never crossed my mind. Anyway, why or how could I?"

"You're a journalist."

"So what?"

"I bet you'd probably sell your granny for a story."

"She's dead. They both are."

"You know what I mean."

"Actually, you've touched a raw nerve. I mean, do you really think all journalists are that bad? Really? Actually, I'd credited you with more intelligence than that."

"Well– "

"Hang on, don't answer. I know what you're thinking, but try and take a broader view. I mean, how many periodicals do you think are published every day, every week and every month in the UK? I'll tell you. Hundreds of thousands, ok? And covering how many subjects? Again, thousands. And how many journalists are there working professionally at any one time in the UK? Do you want to know the answer?" Jenkins asked, charging ahead. "Well, I can't put an exact figure on it, but I think the NUJ has a membership of something like thirty thousand. Ok, so the common perception of journalists is that they are purveyors of salacious gossip and filth who, as you say, would sell their granny for even a half decent story. But tell me now, is that just as true of the deputy editor of *Farmer's Weekly,* say, or the guy who writes the horoscopes for *Woman's Realm* or the problem page for *Practical Woodworking?* No, I don't think so, Peggy. Journalists working on the red tops are just the grubby tip of a pretty clean iceberg. There's plenty of honest hard-grafting journalists working behind the scenes contributing to some very valid publications."

Jenkins stopped and stared thoughtfully at the ground.

"God, that was heartfelt," Peggy Smyth mumbled after a long and awkward pause.

"Yes, it was."

"Do you know something, Dillon?"

"What?"

"I'm not sure you believe that, actually."

"Why not?"

"Because if you believed all that codswallop about journalists offering a useful service, you wouldn't feel the need to bang on about it so much. You probably wouldn't be sitting here, either. You'd be over there, on the other side of that barrier with a notebook and pen and one of those little tape recorders along with all the other newspaper people."

"You know something, you're your brother's sister, all right."

"That's good, 'cos I... I... I like him," she said, with a laugh that sounded so sweet it made him smile too. "Look, Dillon, would you do something for me?" she continued, clasping his hand firmly in her fingers.

"What?"

"Keep an eye on him for me. He's capable of saying or doing almost anything, you know. You'll think he's naive, but actually, it's just that he knows no fear. He has boundless integrity and it's sure to get him into trouble sooner or later, and I think we've all had enough trauma recently."

"I was kind of hoping that *he* would look after *me*."

"Don't worry. I'm sure he will," Peggy said, getting up to go.

"Hang on, there's one thing I'd like to ask you, Peggy."

"What?"

"Has he ever shown any interest in women? Has he ever had a girlfriend?"

Peggy looked stumped.

"God... not for a while. Why?"

"I was just wondering. I can't really imagine it."

"Well... there was *one*."

"There's always one."

"Not so long ago. She was Italian. Broke his heart."

"Well?"

"The Vatican."

"Oh?"

"We have a cousin. A priest. Father Adrian. He was... is... at a seminary in Rome. Ignatius went to visit... well, was sent to visit. Err... I sent him. Anyway, he was kicking his heels around Rome and met an Italian girl. A local. Very beautiful. Maybe not at first glance. Wore glasses. Was beautiful under the glasses. Flavia Briottori. Big hair. Big eyes. Enormous with glasses on. Gentle soul. He didn't come back for two months. Brought her back with him. The sparks were mighty."

"So, what happened?"

"Sad, really. She couldn't speak a word of English. Well, maybe a word."

"And Ignatius couldn't speak– "

"Italian? No."

"Disaster?"

"Well, actually... no. Not really. You see, that was when it worked. I mean, when they couldn't understand a word each other was saying. It was all very mysterious and romantic. They thought the best of each other. It was only when they started to take lessons in English and Italian that things went haywire."

"Really?"

"Yes, really... once they started to converse in each other's language... to really communicate, they realised quite quickly that they had very little in common. They had nothing to say. Whilst before Iggy had appeared dark, brooding and macho, she then realised that he was actually quiet and boring. Well, if not boring, maybe just not her type. And whilst she had seemed to exude sex appeal when he couldn't understand a word *she* said, he then realised that she was manipulative and domineering. Where once he had considered her chattering in Italian, mellifluous and exotic, once translated into English he found her patter shrill and nagging. What had seemed innocent, exciting and romantic fast became a domestic disaster; the worst kind of holiday romance."

159

"So what happened?"

"She fell for a nice Neapolitan boy at her conversational English evening class in Newtownards and went back home with him to Naples. Ignatius just sighed with relief. But he wasn't happy."

"Poor sod. I guess the language of love isn't Italian after all."

"He's still got a thing about Italian girls, though."

"Some chance of finding another one in Fellrock, I suppose."

"Sad, but true... Look, please don't– "

"Say a word? Don't worry."

"Poor Ignatius."

"Italian girls, huh? No wonder he keeps his trap shut."

24

At first light the roundabout resembled a battlefield: a mass of fallen bodies, ragged tents and bivouacs. Banners, flags and pennants flapped like laundry in a tenement yard. Where the peace campaigners couldn't take refuge under canvas or cardboard they were tucked up inside sleeping bags or duvets like giant pupae – purple and pink and lime green. A group slept around the remnants of a camp fire whose cold ashes were blowing across them, turning them Pompeii grey. These were not morning people.

Jenkins tutted, weary following a night filled with guitar jamming, drum thumping and raucous singing in the camp. Slumped against the bollard, he searched his pockets for cigarettes and retrieved a crumpled pack of Marlboros. It was empty save for a half-smoked butt. *Will do,* he thought.

He fired up his Zippo, which he could just about get near enough to catch the tiny butt without burning his nose in the wavering flame. Two deep drags and the fag was done.

He kicked Smyth. Nothing. He kicked him again, but harder.

"*Wa?*"

"Wake up, Smyth."

"*Wa?*"

"Wake up."

"WHAT!"

"How are we going to get rid of these people?"

"Why? What's wrong with them?"

"You know damn well."

"Well," Smyth yawned, "you're the one who craves publicity.

You're the one who said we needed support."

"That's as may be, but I didn't know it would end up attracting this lot."

"I thought you were more egalitarian than that. Anyway, you can't make this thing exclusive. You'll be saying they're the wrong class of people next."

"Yeah ok, Iggy. So I'd like a healthy cross section, but this lot... well, they're not very representative, are they?"

"Ok, ok, hang on. What's really bothering you here?"

"They're probably going to hijack the protest. The substance of what you're doing is going to get obscured by *their* style and *their* politics. The media will take one look at their spiky hair and jumpers and write you off as some kind of fringe lunatic or political extremist."

"Stop worrying about the bloody media. I don't care how I'm portrayed – how this is portrayed. This has got nothing to do with style or appearance."

"You *should* care. If not for your sake then for the sake of what you're trying to achieve."

"Well, I'll tell you what. If their being here matters that much to you, and since you were partly responsible for getting them here, why don't *you* get rid of them?"

Jenkins didn't answer. A ray of sunlight flickering on his eye distracted him. He thought it came from the trees on the far side of the carriageway. It was a glint of light – sun reflected off glass, possibly a camera lens.

Bloody paparazzi, he thought.

The trees were heavy with leaf. Jenkins liked the vivid green; loved green; Ireland's best feature – the green. He reckoned the trees were elms, but couldn't be sure. He thought of his mother. She would know. There was a time when she used to teach him the names of trees, of flowers and birds. He wished he'd paid more attention. Too late. She was gone now.

Jenkins closed his eyes and dozed off, thinking kindly of the elms for the heavy musk they fired into the night air and dreamt

162

of walks through Richmond Park with his mother when he was a child.

High up in an elm tree, a man in black fatigues – Jenkins' photographer – was staring at the ground and hoping the dog circling the trunk below wouldn't pick up his scent and start barking. As he stared, the man considered the received wisdom that the best way to cope with a fear of heights is to never look down. But here he lay staring directly at the foot of the tree without feeling the slightest bit dizzy. It was strange, he thought, how the brain struggled to gauge height. The eighteen or so feet to the ground looked more like forty or forty-five.

When the dark figure looked up to check the sky, however, he felt giddy and disoriented and then tightened his grip. No one ever told you to not look up.

Ribbons of cloud were sailing overhead causing the sun to strobe through the branches above him and making him feel as though the tree were swaying, as if he were lying at the top of a mast, the ship rolling on a stormy sea. Judging by the speed of the clouds the wind was strong at high altitude. He quickly looked back down to regain his balance.

The man considered the wind at ground level. There was only a light breeze. He hoped it wouldn't come into play. He relaxed his grip on the tree. The branch, a main bough, was large and comfortable. It was the width of a pew and had lots of smaller branches growing off it providing leafy camouflage and convenient handholds. He lifted his binoculars to get a better look at the action on the traffic island, but lowered them when he noticed one of the men suddenly look up. The man was staring right back towards him with his hand raised to shield his eyes from the sunlight. Tree man realised his mistake. *Shit! Reflected light!* He should have known better – should have waited for the cloud to pass over again.

Tree man wondered if maybe he'd chosen the wrong vantage point. He knew it was too close to the island, only a couple of hundred yards away, but on the other hand the dense foliage was fine for cover and the undergrowth between the trees and the dual carriageway offered the chance of a quick escape. The knowledge that his equipment allowed him to take the shot from up to a mile away, and that he was risking detection by getting in so close, played on his mind. And now, goddamn it, he had aroused the suspicion of someone known to, and in the company of, his target. He would have to get the job done and get the hell out of there.

A leaf kept flapping against his nose. Tree man snatched at it and then threw it in the air. He watched it spiral to the ground. The leaf didn't waver. Good. The wind wouldn't be a factor. *And excellent! the dog's gone,* he thought.

Looking up again he blew some cool air up the balaclava towards his nose. It was too warm for a balaclava, but it was essential wear on this mission, for camouflage and disguise. It was also the traditional combat dress – such as there was one.

Economising on movement, Thomas McShane slowly raised his weapon till it rested under his chin, then tilted it in his hands until he could look down into the sight. He leaned into the rifle, bracing it between his eye, hands and shoulder, snuggling the stock close to his cheek. He traced a path through the sight, which led across the roundabout, over the tented village, across the road and onto the island, until he found the feet of the man slumped against the bollard. He checked his breathing, taking longer breaths to slow his heart rate and then released any tension lingering in his fingers by flexing them once or twice. He must be calm. He must relax – feel focused.

He ran the sight up and across the man's torso and on past his neck until the concentric circles in the viewfinder crossed the centre of the man's forehead just above the bridge of the nose. McShane was confident that at two hundred yards he could take him out with a single shot to the head. He was close enough and there was no crosswind. One shot. That's all it would take. *A piece of cake.* McShane smiled at the simplicity

164

of his task. Clean and easy and away. The target would know nothing, would feel nothing. Bang! and it would be all over. Lights out. Simple.

As calm as he must be, clear-headed and relaxed, McShane couldn't help but trouble himself with difficult questions. Did he really care so little about this man? Could he really justify killing him? And what would this death achieve, anyway?

But this was probably his last job – Boyce had said as much – so why not just get it done and get out of the way? He wouldn't want to miss the opportunity of bowing out once and for all.

Then, another complication. The target had started talking – was engulfed in conversation – head bobbing, chin wagging.

God, this man can talk for Ireland, McShane thought.

He looked up and glanced over the sight to get a broader view. It was the other character, the large bloke in the mac sitting beside the target; the one who had nearly spotted him. He was waving his arms furiously and gesticulating. He must be winding him up, McShane thought. *What the hell could he be saying that is so contentious?* McShane wished the large bloke would just bugger off. Wished he could have a potshot and take him out first. And he could. And it would be so easy. But no, that would be unprofessional. There had only been one mugshot in the envelope Boyce had given him this time, and there was no mistaking that that was the scruffy guy in the boiler suit.

McShane hadn't needed a photo to identify the target. The face was familiar and for once he could put a name to it: *Ignatius Smyth.* McShane was as aware as any about the sit-down protest on the island – he had been a major player in its conception, after all.

The uneasiness McShane had felt on the way to the 'hit' had by-and-large receded and now that he was primed and ready to go, he had to put any doubts to one side. He summoned the usual sense of detachment. A target was a target. And this was the last one. The last time. Had to be clean.

Time for action. McShane looked down through the sight and checked his breathing again. Checked his grip. Let his right index finger slide along the stock until it found the trigger. Now was the moment. McShane took a slow breath and held it, relaxed his shoulders and fixed the man's forehead in the centre of the viewfinder. He steadied himself and prepared to squeeze the trigger – took one last and deliberate blink to clear his vision. But the blink, a formality, suddenly became a nightmarish hiccup as his right eye – his aiming eye – wouldn't reopen, was jammed shut. Glued-down-eye, the symptom of the pruning injury, had returned to haunt him.

Since McShane's hands were cradling the rifle, he could not rub his eye to encourage it to open. Rather, he shook his head.

Suddenly he felt a rush of air and heard a phizzing sound. Something in flight. At first he thought it must be a bird or a stone, but then the phizz was unmistakable. The phizz of a bullet. A shot from nearby. Or had he fired a loose round in error? Impossible. He lowered his rifle and looked over the sight to the island again. His target had slumped forward and was face down on the paving. McShane strained his good eye looking for blood, but couldn't detect any on or near the man. Not a drop. No, the slump was instinctive – the man had thrown himself forward for protection. The larger man was still on his feet however, but was now sprinting forward. McShane tracked him through the gun sight, as the man ran across to the roundabout. He was running towards the dog. It was the same dog that had been annoying McShane below his elm tree earlier. The large man, whom he recognised as 'Somebody' Jenkins, had reached, and was now crouching over, the dog.

It was the dog then. The dog had been hit. Three of its legs were thrashing as if to run away, but it had been downed, couldn't get up and was frantic. The fourth leg dangled, listless and bright red. There was blood. And people were charging about the island in panic. Some pointed towards the trees.

Enough. Time to go. McShane grasped his rifle under one

arm, rolled over and bailed out of the tree. Falling gently, landing like a bubble. Mission aborted. He stowed his weapon in the tote bag he had previously hidden in the undergrowth.

With a single-minded sense of calm, professional instinct kicked in and drove him along the most direct line of escape. He had a clear vision of his route, having surveyed the possibilities upon arrival. Bus was his preferred transport to the target area, being the most anonymous means – he would try and leave by the same. Merge into a crowd. Any bus, any direction.

As he darted into the undergrowth and was hurdling through bracken, McShane tripped over what he thought was a root. It was only as he tumbled that he saw that the root was wearing a shoe.

McShane rolled onto his haunches and stared back into the foliage. He soon found a face. Camouflaged. Finger-painted in greens and browns. Piercing blue eyes, quite beautiful in their intensity and firing a look that screamed 'Piss off!'. The crouching figure, a man, grimaced for extra emphasis. He was gripping a rifle. A lazy plume of smoke was rising from the barrel and a telltale whiff of cordite hung in the air. McShane was relieved that, indeed, he hadn't fired a round by accident. Taking a deep breath to steady his nerves, he saw that the gun was not standard army issue, but thought that the man's flak jacket was.

"Why the dog?" McShane whispered.

The man stared back, silent, then nodded towards the undergrowth. McShane understood. He wouldn't be getting an answer. He grabbed the tote bag and took off.

"You *eejit*! You missed, didn't ya? Fucking useless twat!" McShane shouted, laughing loudly as he ran.

But he knew, or thought he knew. Shooting the dog was a warning. Scare tactics to put the wind up the protesters. Typical of the Brits. The dirty tricks brigade. The army weren't out to kill this time, just frighten. And to the Brits, the dogs of this war were dispensable. He remembered how they had poisoned his mother's dog. Well, had been suspected of it, anyway. The family had found it by the back door. Dead.

"Barking dogs blow cover, especially when you're crawling around suburban gardens," he remembered his father saying.

Expecting a bullet to phizz his way at any moment, McShane bolted.

Cradling his rifle, Lexy Danvers watched McShane's progress through the bracken until he disappeared from view. Danvers wouldn't have thought too kindly of being mistaken for a British soldier. He thought himself above that. And he would have pursued McShane, hunted him down, knifed him, garrotted him or just strangled him with his bare hands, but couldn't move now. His heart was beating healthily enough, but pumping too much blood too quickly, through an artery torn open by the RUC bullet that had winged him as he was fleeing the barn at Kilcarron.

Danvers knew enough first aid to apply a tourniquet at the time he was shot and had had the wound stitched by a Shankill doctor soon after. But the wound had snagged on a branch and reopened when Danvers was dragging himself up into a tree to get a vantage point overlooking the island.

Once in the tree he had had barely enough energy to raise his gun, train it in on Dillon Jenkins and pull the trigger, but not nearly enough energy to direct the bullet with the accuracy required. Now, light-headed and slumped on his knees in the bracken, Danvers' head rolled down to rest on his chest as a stream of blood pulsed across the bright green ferns.

Half stumbling, half running, McShane hadn't looked round until he cleared the undergrowth on the far side of the copse. He ripped off his balaclava, stuffed it in his pocket, then vaulted the fence into the rugby club car park. There he mingled with the crowd milling about the vans and assorted vehicles that had arrived with the peace convoy. He slowed to a stroll, his sports bag slung casually over one shoulder, ambling with deliberate calmness to subdue his heartbeat, not wanting to appear agitated. He made his way past the clubhouse and down the drive, walking slowly, attempting to portray innocence by way of a dawdle.

As he neared the front entrance McShane noticed a mauve Ford straddling the footpath beside the main road into Ballyblessington, its engine running. There was something about the angle at which it had been parked, something about the revving of the engine that seemed sinister. McShane's instincts told him that there was something amiss, but still the car had to be negotiated. As he sauntered past on the passenger side, he bent forward to take a peek through the window at the driver and immediately recognised the polka-dotted complexion of Michael, his teenage accomplice from the Antrim Road job.

McShane would have ignored the kid and carried on with the short walk into Ballyblessington, but for the appearance of an RUC Land Rover accelerating towards them over the dip in the road, siren blaring. It roared past, heading for the roundabout behind him.

Soon the soundscape was thick with the wail of sirens coming from all directions.

"What the– "

"For God's sake, get in McShane."

McShane would have loved to have laid one on the kid, but knew that this was neither the time nor the place.

"Ok, Michael. Get me the hell out of here," McShane said with calm authority, as he slumped onto the passenger's seat. He threw his head back and breathed a sigh of relief.

"Sure," the kid grunted, but turned off the ignition with his right hand whilst raising a pistol with his left. The gun was cumbersome and difficult to handle in the confined space with a silencer attached.

"What the– "

McShane's face drained to white.

"You're an idiot, McShane. Why can't you follow orders?" a familiar voice growled from the back of the car.

"Boyce! You weren't hiding from me, were you?" McShane sneered as Boyce rose up from behind the front seats.

"Drive on Michael," Boyce commanded, taking the gun and ramming it against McShane's right kidney.

"Anyway, what orders?" McShane asked, trying to ignore the discomfort from the gun in his side.

"You must think you're a cut above the rest of us, McShane," Boyce said, ignoring the question.

"What?"

"There's no stopping you, is there? You're out of control, Tommy."

"I'm sorry, you've lost me."

"You've become a liability. Times have changed."

"Look, I haven't got a clue what you're talking about, Boyce."

"Are you really that much out of touch? Do you really have no idea what's going on any more? You've been stood down, you idiot. We're announcing a ceasefire tonight. An end to hostilities. You weren't supposed to turn up here today. Your party was cancelled. Didn't you get the message, McShane?"

"What message?"

"We tried to tell you. But of course you've gone to ground. We couldn't find you. As I say. You've become a bit of a problem. A renegade. There's no stopping you, McShane. We have no use for psychopaths like you... we don't need your type any more."

"God, Boyce– "

"The political struggle's started. People like you are a liability now."

"What do you mean, 'people like me'?"

"Mad dogs, McShane. Killers. Your day has passed. I tried to tell you. I tried to warn you."

"Well, I couldn't have been listening or you weren't trying too hard, because I've heard nothing."

"Exactly."

"Well, try me now, Boyce. I hear what you're saying."

"It's too late, McShane. As I say, you're a liability. We don't need psychos. It's a pity, but there you go."

McShane knew there was no arguing with the man. He feared what was to come, but felt a strange sense of acceptance.

He heard the ear-splitting crack when Boyce fired the gun, but immediately passed out without feeling any pain. Smoke meandered from the barrel of Boyce's pistol. One shot. McShane's head had fallen sideways and was smearing blood down the passenger's side window, his face locked in surprise – raised eyebrows and glassy eyes.

The car sped on cross-country. McShane was still slumped against the window, his face contorted into the grotesque expression of a gargoyle – eyes fixed on the passing verge, his stare exaggerated by the glass, with nose flattened and lips spreading across the pane like the backside of a water snail on a fish tank.

At dusk, Boyce and the boy Michael drove McShane out to the city dump. It was a desolate area on the edge of the Belfast Harbour Estate near the lough shore, strewn with waste paper and plastic bags. The mauve Ford bumped and bobbled out along a mud track studded with broken glass. When they felt that they were far enough away from civilisation not to attract attention, they rolled the body onto a pile of bin bags before making a hurried exit. As they walked back to the car they wiped their hands on their trousers to rid themselves of McShane's blood. The stolen car would be torched later.

25

A scream came like a starting pistol. As soon as the shot was fired and the dog felled, panic became endemic as people dashed around like ants avoiding boiling water. Duty policemen and women were galvanised by DI Williams who dispatched half a dozen to make an assault on the trees in front of the rugby club.

When he reached the dog, Jenkins' trembling fingers quickly located the wound. The bullet had punched a hole in the dog's front leg, high up near the shoulder. To his relief he found an exit wound. Blood was oozing over the fur leaving it matted and sticky. The dog looked dead, but Jenkins could feel its heart racing. He guessed the dog was out cold from the shock. He pressed his hand hard against the wound to stem the bleeding.

"Call for an ambulance!" he screamed at the pressmen. "And stop those bastards taking photographs!"

"There's no way they'll send one for a dog, Dillon!"

"Then say it's for me. Say anything. Just get me a bloody ambulance. What's this dog ever done to harm anybody? Who would do this, for God's sake?"

"Maybe it was an avenging postman. How the hell would I know?" Smyth replied.

Jenkins had got used to Smyth's cynicism and found it oddly reassuring. Like a dock leaf, it drew the sting out of almost any situation.

The chain of events appeared to be passing in either fast or slow motion and blurring Jenkins' grasp on reality. Soon the roundabout had drained of bystanders, cleared out of the line of fire by a policeman squawking *"Stand back! Stand back!"* through a loudhailer, with the intonation of a Dalek.

As the public fled the junction, police reinforcements sprinted past to take up positions on the roundabout and then, using the ragtag tents as cover, they joined the advance towards the trees with pistols drawn.

Jenkins was sitting on the ground cross-legged, with the injured dog lying across his lap. Smyth sat beside him stroking the dog's head. A dramatic tableau, the eye in a storm of forest-green, as swarms of armed police ran past.

And then there were sirens and bellowed orders.

"Stand clear! Stand clear!"

And people running. And more shouting. And voices crackling on radios.

"Do you need the military? Over."

And panic.

"Where's the bloody ambulance?"

And mayhem.

"Can't get through."

But eventually the madness calmed; the shouting and sirens giving way to the gentler buzz of nervous chatter.

And a vet was found.

The search for the gunman continued. Some people reported seeing a man in dark clothes clambering over a fence. He was of average height and might have had brown eyes, but then again, they might have been green. No distinguishing features. Oh, except for a slight hump – small, almost undetectable, but there all right.

The search was called off when they found Lexy Danvers sitting on his haunches, upright, eyes wide open, but the blood fast congealing in his veins, his frame stiffening as rigor mortis set in.

Soon order regained a foothold on the day and Jenkins and Smyth returned to their spot beside the bollard.

Jenkins was preoccupied with worry about the dog, but it was a preoccupation that annoyed him. He kept telling himself that to care so much for the plight of an animal, a pet, when there had been so many human victims of the troubles, was almost immoral. It reminded him of the furore caused by the bomb attack on the Horse Guards in Hyde Park in the early eighties when the press and public seemed more upset by the injuries to the horses than the death of the men.

No one knew where the dog was from; it just always seemed to be there. An omen. A lucky charm. Jenkins liked the dog's independence; it was a loner like himself.

"You can't stay here forever, gentlemen, I'm afraid," DI Williams told them in a well-mannered voice, mellow and honeyed. He'd removed his cap and was in the midst of applying himself to a 'softly, softly' approach.

"Well, I'm afraid we're going to stay. Why should we move? Just because some idiot in the woods is firing guns at us? Anyway he's gone," Jenkins said, sounding a note of defiance.

"'Scuse me, sir. I think you should listen to this," a young policeman in plain clothes said, interrupting the detective inspector, and ushering him to one side.

Their conversation was brief. Jenkins could hear enough detail to get the picture.

"It'll be on the radio, sir. The hourly news..."

The young officer turned on the pocket-sized transistor he was holding.

"In response to what it referred to as 'positive political developments', the IRA announced an unconditional ceasefire this morning..."

"Bloody hell!"

"The statement came just after 11.00 hours BST and stated that there would be a 'complete cessation of military operations' from midnight tonight and that the terrorist organisation was now willing to enter into inclusive talks on the political future of the Province. The statement has raised hopes

for a lasting peace and an end to twenty-five years of bombing and shooting..."

"Peace?" Jenkins asked, looking at Smyth in disbelief.

"Who knows? We've been here before."

"...British Prime Minister, John Major, was cautious in his reaction to the IRA announcement. 'We are beyond the beginning,' he said, 'but we are not yet in sight of the end...'"

"What do you think *we* should do, Smyth?"

"Sit and wait."

"That'll make a change."

26

Peggy Smyth had witnessed the shooting; seen the thrashing legs, the pool of blood, Jenkins cradling the dog. She was hoovering at the time. Lapping the sitting room in Fellrock in ever decreasing circles. The TV was on in the background and caught her attention. No sound, but the pictures spoke volumes. The shooting had been on the lunchtime news, live footage fed straight to the studio. The shaky hand-held camerawork, the crazed people rushing about with panic-stricken faces, confirmed Peggy Smyth's worst fears.

She stood rooted, jaw agape, the Hoover squealing like a pig on the carpet at her feet. By the time she had the wit to switch off the machine, the report was ending.

"...many of whom are now expressing concern for the safety of the two men cast away on this small desert island outside Fellrock. Philip Park... Lunchtime News... County Down..."

The bulletin cut to a report of an arson attack on a house in Magherafelt.

Peggy Smyth switched the Hoover back on with her toe and pushed it across the floor, too shocked and too determined to consider abandoning her task. But then she had second thoughts and stamped on the 'off' button before she had forced the machine to travel much further than a couple of yards. Anyway, she thought she'd heard something. The doorbell. She had. It rang again.

"Yes?"

"Hello Miss Smyth... It's only me... Andrew Craddick."

"Mr Craddick!"

"I thought I should come."

Craddick extended a palm, which Peggy Smyth stared at blankly. The hand was withdrawn.

"Can you spare me a moment, Miss Smyth?"

"It's *Ms* Smyth, actually. Erm, I'm afraid you haven't picked a very good time, Mr Craddick. Haven't you heard?"

"Exactly. I feel there's not a moment to lose, *Ms* Smyth."

"What– "

"Do you mind if I come in?"

Craddick was already halfway across the lounge. He had irritated Peggy by omitting to wipe his feet and was now leaving a trail of dried mud across the carpet.

"Ms Smyth, they need our help."

"*Our* help?"

"Exactly."

"But– "

"Shooting or no, Ms Smyth, I wanted to see you this morning. Though the shooting does underline the danger I believe your brother to be in."

"*Danger?* What are you talking about?"

"Look, I've got something to put to you. A plan."

"Err, one moment, Mr Craddick. Your timing is – to say the least – not the best today," Peggy said, a little testily. "Three things. Firstly: what can you possibly do to help? Secondly: what makes you think I'm interested in your 'plan'? And thirdly... well, actually... there isn't a 'thirdly'."

"Exactly. There is no 'thirdly'. That's why they need my help. They need a plan 'C'."

"As I say, your timing isn't great, Mr Craddick."

"Look, Ms Smyth, I've thought for some time that they are getting out of their depth – that they might be in danger. I hear things, Ms Smyth."

"You can get tablets for that, Mr Craddick."

"No, seriously, I hear rumours, Ms Smyth. I've heard that

they are ruffling feathers. I hear they are on lists. They are being targeted."

"Well, that's pretty obvious judging from the fracas this morning."

"Look, to cut a long story short, I've found them a safe haven."

"A what?"

"Somewhere safe. Somewhere where they can protest in peace."

"I don't think you quite understand my brother, Mr Craddick. Are you sure you know what you're getting into?"

"Yes, absolutely. Please, let me explain– "

"There's no need, Mr Craddick. Look, let me make this easy for you... my brother will not be leaving his island. End of story."

"But– "

"Are you listening? He's going nowhere, Mr Craddick."

"He can't stay there, Ms Smyth."

"That's not for you to say."

"But he– "

"It's none of your business, Mr Craddick.'

"But– "

Stretching to her full height, Peggy Smyth bore down on the solicitor with such bravado that he found himself shuffling backwards towards the door.

"Please, Ms Smyth! One moment."

"Come on now. Out you go."

"Please, Ms Smyth! Just look and read."

Craddick thrust forward a letter, fending off Peggy Smyth as if she were a vampire and the sheet of paper and its envelope a crucifix. Peggy stalled.

"It's from Belfast City Council. They want to make Ignatius an offer. There's a proposal."

Peggy Smyth snatched the letter, took a cursory glance, then held it more firmly and read on, sitting down onto the bottom step of the staircase as she did so.

"They'll never go for this, you know," she said, folding the note.

"They might, Ms Smyth. They might," Craddick said, gaining in confidence. "They should at least consider it. I really think they... No look, I'll leave it with you."

Craddick backed out of the door, bowed and then pulled it shut behind him with the gentlest of thuds.

27

From the depths of unconsciousness, Thomas Eugene McShane's brain suddenly clicked into gear. He awoke with immediate clarity followed by an overwhelming sense of relief and a euphoria for life – a positive perspective that had eluded him for years. He hadn't felt this positive since... since when? The first month or two when he'd met his wife? God, how excited they were then. Everything they did and said was riven with energy – raw and fresh.

When they met, he thought all his Christmases had come in one month. She consumed him with her vitality and passion. He'd never known excitement like it, or anyone like her. It had all seemed so natural and so right. He hadn't had to do much; she chose him. He was her man. Simple.

He'd been an innocent bystander, sipping a pint in the Harbour Bar, Sheephaven Bay, Donegal. She picked him out from the crowd. Teased him, tickled his fancy, bedded him, married him, but now had left him broken and broke.

He smiled when he remembered his wife's initial enthusiasm, then the transition from girlfriend to wife, and laughed when he remembered her attempts at domesticity as she tried to cook up a storm.

They had holidayed in Portstewart in the early years. A calm port during troubled times in Belfast. But rainy. They would shelter in Morelli's and gorge on ice cream. A 'Nuts Galore' was his preferred sundae. She *must* have loved him then... she stretched her culinary skills to imitate the dish at home. A mountain of chocolate sauce, hazelnuts and vanilla ice cream.

A poor imitation, but well meant. Now he frowned and wondered.

Flat on his back McShane scanned the sky, which shimmered a pale blue, undiluted by patches of grey and uninterrupted by even the slightest hint of a breeze. Days like this were rare in Northern Ireland and savoured when they came; barbecue weather. McShane wondered where he was. But wherever it was, it didn't smell too fresh. He tried a deep breath to search for the scent of burning charcoal, but his lungs wouldn't allow it – he coughed. And his nose was clogged with what he imagined was dried blood.

He couldn't see very far in either direction. What view he had was dominated by mounds of bin bags – as if he were lying in some kind of giant open-air laundry. But then a pile of washing has softer contours, and, unless somehow soiled, a sweeter fragrance. The lumps and bumps of the black bags beneath and the squawking of the crows hopping around him, were obvious clues. And McShane would have stood for a better view of the Belfast City dump, but was too exhausted and sensed a lack of mobility in his legs anyway. Had he been able to stand and clamber to a vantage point, the view would have startled him. He would have gasped at the debris – a vast ocean of garbage stretching far into the distance.

Everywhere refuse bags had been torn open by rodents, the contents tipping out through the slashed plastic. The dump was a poor man's zoo, the habitat of the wildlife of Greater Belfast. The inmates came and went as they pleased.

A rat shot across McShane's chest, scurrying away when startled by his shallow breathing. McShane would have taken a swipe at it, but found he could move neither his arms nor his hands. He had already tried flexing his fingers and toes but couldn't tell if they'd moved because he couldn't see or feel them. The predominance of his sensory awareness manifested itself as a pain centred in his head from the neck up. He also found it hard to swallow, which was distressing, but it was the headache which was causing the most discomfort. It was constant, nagging and sharp, as if somebody had drilled a hole in the top of his head and was now screwing in a bolt. Agony. And yet he felt euphoric just to be there; to be alive when he knew he should be dead.

Before long a seagull drifted into view, hanging effortlessly on a thermal high overhead. It reminded him of the drive along the motorway from Newtownabbey to Belfast. Often he would catch a glimpse of seagulls flying into the wind down Belfast Lough, struggling out to sea but getting nowhere; never moving, just hovering, always struggling. And he'd feel like shouting at them, "Give it up you stupid bastards! Please, please, just give it up!"

And why the hell did they fly head-on into the wind when for all the effort they could only just about stay where they were without being blown backwards? The waste of energy and sheer pointlessness made his flesh creep, like the screech of a knife on china. No progress, absolutely no progress. The only comfort that his imagination could offer him was that they might be training; building up their strength for a great escape across the Irish Sea on a calmer day. But for all that the seagulls annoyed him, he understood and chuckled; reassured that he wasn't alone in banging his head against a brick wall.

The gull overhead drifted off. McShane tried to turn his head to follow its progress, but couldn't and so watched it through the corner of his good eye till it was gone. His bad eye wasn't working today – was glued shut. He had a feeling that this time it might not be opening again. The only bits of him that would budge now were his left eye and his epiglottis as he fought to swallow.

Then he had company. He had closed his good eye for a second – a long blink to try and squeegee away the film of weepy goo challenging his focus on the sky – but then, when the eye cleared, he could see the ghostly figure of Colin Downey looming before him, silent and haunting, looking down on him, hovering in the sky just about where the seagull had been.

"Eff away off, Downey. Go on, bugger off! You don't bloody scare me. Anyway, I'll be joining you before this day's out, so you'd better be good to me now. Go on, piss off!"

But Colin Downey just stared back through his surviving eye.

"Bloody hell, Downey... we've not got a pair of eyes between us."

But the apparition did not smile.

"Ok, Downey. Out with it! What the hell do you want?"

McShane was shouting, but slurring his words as if drunk.

Colin Downey stared back.

"What do you want?"

Colin Downey just kept on staring.

"What do you want me to say? 'Sorry' or something? Well you're a figment of my imagination, so you know I'm sorry. And anyway, you know it was a fucking accident. What the hell were you doing there in the first place? Why weren't you at home? What was a ten-year-old doing hanging round an army checkpoint at nine o'clock at night for, anyway?"

And still Colin Downey just stared back.

"Oh, for God's sake Colin, just open your bloody mouth and say something."

McShane tried turning his head away, but his neck still wasn't for twisting. He tried shutting the good eye, but it now seemed to be stuck open in contrast to the one that was stuck shut. And there was Colin Downey, hovering in the sky like an angel, reminding McShane of the portraits on the football cards he used to collect as a kid: 'A&BC Gum's First Division Players 1970/71 season'. The footballers often seemed to be looking down into the camera, such was their height, and the photos were often retouched to give them a lurid Day-Glo sky – a turquoise tint which was dropped in behind the head and shoulders; very surreal. Just like the vision of Colin Downey.

But suddenly Downey made a noise, or tried to. McShane saw

the mouth open and shut. Just a slight movement, but he saw it all right.

"Pardon, Colin?"

Then nothing. Just silence and a long pause.

"Look, Colin, if you've got something to tell me you'd better get on with it, because I can't guarantee that I'll be around for too much longer."

More silence. But McShane detected movement in the mouth again. Then there came a groan. A long expelling of air. A slow guttural sound like a moan. Like a man moaning, quite deep and mature, not the sound of a ten-year-old. The mouth moved, making the moan change in pitch and volume.

"Bloody hell, Colin, spit it out!"

"WER WER... WER WER..." Colin moaned, the volume rising. And now, over and over, "WER WER... WER WER..."

"Look, I'm sorry Colin... *Wer Wer... Wer Wer...* what does it mean? You're going to have to help me out here."

"MERVER MERVER..." Colin mumbled – low and gravelly.

"*Merver?* What the hell is that, Colin?" McShane shouted, then paused. Then a realisation. "It's your mother, isn't it, Colin?"

Colin stared back, silent.

"Oh God! It is, isn't it? It's your mother. Well ok, Colin... your mother. You want me to say sorry to your mother, is that it? Well ok, I would... I'd love to, but how the hell can I? How the hell can I say sorry to your mother when I'm stuck in this bloody place?"

"MERVER!" Colin groaned back, louder and more agitated.

"All right, Colin! Ok, I am sorry. And Mrs Downey, wherever you are, I am sorry. I am sorry I accidentally shot Colin. And Colin, I am sorry I shot you too... but, I mean, look at me. How is this going to help you now?"

"MERVER!"

"Ok, ok, I'm sorry. I am fucking sorry! But one of us is dead, one of us is dying and the one that matters isn't here, Colin. I'm sorry... I *am* very very sorry. Colin, I am truly fucking sorry, but what can I do?"

Overhead the seagull soared, riding high on another thermal. It scanned the sea of black bin liners, broken chairs and waste paper for signs of food. It was aware of the body lying on the bed of bin bags below and could make out detail in its face. It could even detect a slight movement in the man's left eye, but it meant nothing to the bird, however, when the eye slowly closed, its spark extinguished; nor could it comprehend the frail voice whispering over and over, *"God loves me too, Colin. God loves me too..."*

28

The dog reappeared about a week after the shooting. Its injured leg was bandaged, forcing it to hobble along on the other three as best it could. Round its neck it wore a plastic cone to stop it chewing at the dressing. It looked like the dog on the old His Master's Voice label, but with its head rammed up the horn of the gramophone instead of looking into it. It wobbled onto the traffic island from the direction of the town.

Smyth and Jenkins didn't notice at first. They were too busy arguing. It was only when the row reached a crescendo and they disengaged for a moment or two to sulk, that they noticed the dog lying beside them, panting heavily whilst waiting patiently for attention.

"Agh!" Smyth screamed.

"For God's sake, Dog! Don't do that!" Jenkins stammered, also jumping out of his skin.

Having made a fuss of the dog they sat down to re-engage.

"You're a bloody fool, Jenkins. You know that, don't you? A bloody fool. I mean, that stupid bloody scarf you're wearing..."

"The Dalai Lama's?"

"The Dalai Lama's, my arse. And you think *I'm* gullible. The Dalai Lama... do you know where your scarf's from? A flea-market. Nutts bloody Corner."

"How the hell would you know?"

"Because it's the kind of cheap tat you find there, nestling between the boxes of dodgy videos and fake aftershave."

Jenkins untied the turquoise scarf and slowly pulled it away from his neck as if he were lowering the flag at a closing ceremony.

"Nutts Corner? You could have told me, Smyth. There are photos of me wearing this shite all over the place."

"Serves you bloody well right then, you vain twat."

It had only taken a week following the shooting for the squabbling to resume. There had been an uneasy peace between them for days in the interim, however. In the aftermath of the IRA's announcement of a ceasefire came endless questions from the press angling for a story. Since Smyth and Jenkins had become advocates for peace, it was only natural that they were sought out to endorse the ceasefire and give an opinion on the politicking that followed. It was already being coined the 'Peace Process'.

"If I see another turquoise silk scarf this side of Christmas, I'll use it to throttle someone, so I will!" Smyth moaned.

"Your cheap scarf is the least of our problems," Jenkins murmured.

"What do you mean?"

"You know."

"What?"

"The climate. The political one. You can't tell me you're a hundred per cent happy about the way things are heading."

"Well to be honest, it's hard to differentiate between the implications for the province – which look abso-bloody-lutely marvellous, the implications for our protest – which look abso-bloody-lutely catastrophic, and the implications for us personally which look... well... just confusing. And I am, indeed... very confused."

"No you're not."

"I am."

"No you're not."

"Bloody am."

"Look, Smyth, you're not. It's simple. You hate the ceasefire. Hate it. It's going to totally disenfranchise you."

"That's ridiculous!"

"Is it? Right. Ok. You hate the ceasefire, because it means that you're going to have to leave the island and rejoin the rat race. You'll have to look for a job, mate. You'll hate that. I mean what are you going to do? Go back to tyre fitting?"

"Well, there's not much chance of that."

"What?"

"Me, going back to the tyres."

"Yes, and you're not the only one. I mean, if it sticks – if the ceasefire holds – can you imagine all those hard men: the hit men, the extortionists, the racketeers, the bombers and the gun-runners enrolling down at their local job centre?"

"I don't really care what they do. I'll still be sitting here."

"You crazy?"

"Yes. And you know I am."

"Why? What's the point? The job's done, mate. The fighting's stopped."

"Well, there's more than just our local perspective to consider. I mean, just because those guys in the betting office were Northern Irish and victims of the Northern Irish troubles, and just because I'm Northern Irish and our sit-down is located in Northern Ireland, doesn't mean to say that our protest doesn't have an international dimension. I mean, you're not Northern Irish, most of the reporters, photographers and film crews aren't from here. Does that matter? Does that invalidate what we are doing? Our peace protest supersedes local issues. Not that I'm saying the troubles are just a local issue. I don't want to be disrespectful, but what I'm really saying is that our protest is for peace *everywhere*, not just in Northern Ireland. We are a constant reminder of what has been and why we should all strive to make the peace work – to maintain the peace. Who says this ceasefire's going to hold, anyway? They haven't before. The republicans and the loyalists are still armed up to their back teeth and the politicians haven't started talking across the divide."

"Have faith, man. Have a little optimism."

"To my mind, there are something like four thousand dead Northern Irish men and women who would say 'no' to optimism."

"Well, maybe the one million still alive want to say 'yes'."

"This is premature."

"It always is, Smyth. You can't move a pony and cart by pushing it from behind. You've got to get on board and drive."

"Obviously. What the hell do you think we've been doing here all spring and summer?"

"Look, Smyth, all I'm saying is that the box office takings are down. The level of interest in what we're doing here is waning. Look about you, for God's sake. Where's everybody gone? You're getting to be old news, man."

They sat in silence for a minute or two until Jenkins got to his feet, turned towards Smyth and began slow handclapping.

"Bravo! Brilliant. Quite brilliant. You're not going to move, are you? You're stuck, yeah? Stranded. Stranded here on your desert island with nowhere to go? And this is your life now, isn't it, Ignatius? Sitting on a traffic island, watching the world go by – and you can't move. Even if you wanted to, you can't move, because you're stuck. You being here isn't really a protest at all, is it? Bloody hell. It's so obvious now. That's just a cover, isn't it? Hell! It's got nothing to do with the shooting. That's just an excuse. Nothing to do with a protest for peace at all. Amazing! And you've got us all believing you. You're not really protesting, you just can't face life in the twentieth century, can you? God, that's sad, man. I'm glad I've found you out at last."

"Look, you bastard, A. you couldn't be more wrong, B. don't patronise me, and C. I can leave this place any time I want to."

"*Bollocks*!"

"No. You'll see."

"What the hell am I going to see?"

"How this protest is going to have influence – ceasefire or no."

"I'm sorry, Smyth, but you're talking crap. You're only going to have influence now if you do something dramatic like pour five gallons of kerosene over your head and set fire to it or get hold of a gun and run amok through Ballyblessington shooting OAPs and traffic wardens. Face it, your time has passed, mate. News moves on."

"Well, yours would be a serious and worrying opinion, Jenkins, if I took anything you said seriously. Words like 'impact' and 'influence', that's just the kind of babble that media people like you speak. In the immortal words of Doris Day, 'Whatever will be, will be'. You see, you can't control the news and you can't control us. You and your kind like to tell us when to start listening and when to stop. But you can't make the news, however hard you try and you make a mistake by trying to stage-manage it. You still present the news in terms of white hats versus black hats, good versus evil, but life is more complex – more organic – than goodies and baddies and right versus wrong."

"You're missing the point."

"Am I?"

"Actually, you're beginning to lose *me*, Smyth. I'm just trying to point out that maybe it's time to pack up and go home – to get a life. We've had our day here."

"By your standards, yes. By your standards this is old news. But not by mine. I'm staying. It serves a function."

"It's your call, but, as I say, I've got a feeling you're stuck here and I've got a feeling you're going to be overtaken by events. And when history moves on, I don't think this is going to be a pleasant place to be."

Smyth stood up and got close to Jenkins, his face only a few inches away. He could feel the warmth of Jenkins' breath.

"You think you're pretty smart, don't you?" Smyth asked, in almost a whisper. "You think you've got me, this and everything and everybody else sussed. Yes, and in your own way you probably have. Maybe yours are modern standards and represent modern thinking, but they're not mine. I believe in something else."

"What?"

"I believe in loyalty, consistency, honesty, compassion and respect, for a start."

"And?"

"And The Ten Commandments."

"The *what*?" Jenkins roared, turning away.

"The Commandments."

"*Thou shalt not worship false idols?*" Jenkins guffawed.

"Make that nine, then. Whatever. Check 'em out sometime, pal."

"You really are on another planet."

"Well, that's just typical of what you would say. Actually, I thought I could count on you for your support."

"You can. Up to a point."

"What about this then?"

Smyth pulled a rolled-up copy of the *Telegraph* from the pocket at the front of his overalls. It took a few seconds for him to rifle through the pages to find what he was looking for. Then he unfolded the double page feature and spread it out on the pavement at Jenkins' feet.

"Yours, I believe," Smyth said, looking up.

The feature bore the headline: *Life as the Fellrock Two. An exclusive story by Dillon Jenkins.*

There was silence as Jenkins searched for words.

"I'll tell you what that is, Ignatius– "

"Oh, I can't wait to hear this."

"It's great publicity. By now that article's been syndicated around the world. Millions more people now know about what you're doing here for peace."

"That's what *you* want to believe. But this hasn't been and isn't about *you*. Anyway, we diverge. You lied. You told me that you'd been sacked. You obviously weren't."

"Ok. Well, I'm sorry about that– "

"You're not bloody sorry. I can see it in your face. It's part of your way of life. You're a professional liar. It's ingrained. You're not sorry at all. Look me in the eye and tell me that you really don't believe that lying is a legitimate means. Anyway, I knew you were a liar."

"I'm not– "

"Of course you are. You're trained to lie. You'd say anything if you thought it would get you a story. You'd do it again tomorrow – especially for an exclusive."

"Hasn't it ever occurred to you that some of those people whose stories we print actually want us to do it?"

"Well– "

"No, of course not. That would never cross your mind. Well, do you know what happened during my first week as a junior on a daily newspaper? No, you don't. I'll tell you. Bhopal... the gas cloud in India, right? How many died? I don't know. I forget... thousands. But do you know what I heard (maybe it was my second, maybe my third day at work)? I heard the news reporter sitting behind me talking to a victim's relative on the phone, all the way from whatever far-flung province Bhopal is in in India– "

"Madhya Pradesh."

"Is it? Amazing! Anyway, the reporter couldn't write down the words fast enough to keep up with the relative's account. And do you know why the relative was so keen to give the story to the newspaper? Because they wanted the world to know about their plight. About the injustice. They wanted to expose the chemical company – the government bungling – whatever. I can't remember the detail, but they wanted maximum exposure because, as they saw it, it was one way – a small way – of honouring their dead and helping to prevent anything similar happening again."

"Very moving. Is this supposed to impress me? Am I now

supposed to believe that your actions in writing this feature were noble?"

"I don't know, but maybe it helps you understand my world a little more."

"Look, as I said, this isn't about you. *You* came to *me*. I never invited you to listen to my story. I never told you my story. You just came and sat down with me and then stole it. You could have asked, but you didn't. Anyway, I don't need to understand your world. As I said to you before, you're either on my side or against me. You lied to me. You are going to profit by this story, which is more than can be said for the dependents of the eight shot dead in the bookies'. Looks like you're against me now. But I'll let you into a secret."

"What?"

"You didn't break my trust."

"Oh, come on."

"And do you want to know why?"

"Why?"

"I'll tell you... because I never trusted you in the first place. I saw you coming, mate!"

Jenkins put an arm on Smyth's shoulder. A conciliatory gesture. Smyth shrugged it off.

"Don't fucking patronise me!" he snarled, leaning forward with a fierce look in his eye. If he had had hackles, they would have risen.

"Do you know something, Smyth? Your sanctimonious attitude is really starting to piss me off too. Holier than thou? There's no one quite as fucking holy as you, mate. You'd make God feel self-conscious. What can any of us do, to do right by you?"

Jenkins' nostrils were flaring.

"Right. Come on, come on then. If I annoy you that much, take a swing. Come on, let's see what you're really made of, Jenkins, you big lump of blubber!"

The two were bent forward like sumo wrestlers on the brink

of combat and locked in an ugly stare. Smyth beckoned Jenkins on with a vigorous flapping of his hands. Next would come a punch, a wild swing, a haymaker.

They were frozen on the barren landscape of the island, their aggressive display drawing the attention of passers-by beyond the police barriers. Meanwhile the last of the press photographers leaned forward, ready to record what promised to be a newsworthy twist in the tale.

A stalemate. Slowly Jenkins reached down and picked up the copy of the paper just as the prevailing breeze began to whip at its pages, threatening to blow them across the road. He screwed the newsprint up into a ball and was about to hurl it at Smyth when a group of the campaigners – the original delegation of three – approached from the roundabout.

Embarrassed and shamed into regaining a sense of decorum, Jenkins stood up straight and beamed an awkward smile whilst ramming the scrunched-up newspaper into his coat pocket.

The deputation stepped onto the traffic island and gathered before them wearing broad innocent smiles.

"We've come to say goodbye. We're leaving. We've decided to set off early tomorrow," the ginger-haired English boy announced.

"O-O-Oh, right," Jenkins stuttered in surprise, his cheeks flushed. "Why?"

"Where are you going next?" Smyth asked in a friendly tone.

"Probably Wales," the second one with glasses said with enthusiasm. "Well, definitely Wales. We're going to catch the ferry for Holyhead tomorrow in Dublin and then lie low in Pembrokeshire for a while. There's plenty of space for us there and we won't be bothering anybody. We'll see."

"We kind of feel that the job's done here, you know?" the first one added.

The group shook hands and exchanged hugs. The deputation retreated to the roundabout, where the packing had already begun.

"So, why didn't you take *them* to task, Ignatius? Why didn't you give *them* a hard time about deserting the cause? Is it because they're not journalists, by any chance?"

"What the hell is your problem? They're just kids. They can do what the hell they like. That's freedom for you. You're different. You're a grown man. It's time you did something with your life, Jenkins."

"And you call sitting beside a traffic bollard 'doing something with your life'?"

"Yes."

"Seriously?"

"Yes. It's a sacrifice."

"Really?"

"Yes. For peace."

"But everybody is deserting you. Soon there'll just be you and me. Doesn't that tell you something?"

"Look, I don't care. All I care about is being here. It's quite simple."

"Really?"

"Yes."

Jenkins sat back down. The two of them sat beside the bollard like bookends, the dog at their feet.

"Iggy?"

"What?"

"I'm sorry about the article."

"No you're not."

29

What Dillon Jenkins liked most about the Smyth house in Fellrock was the quiet. It also seemed civilised – was calm. It smelled right and had a happy disposition. The kitchen was its hub. Tea and Hob Nobs were now the fuel of conversation.

"So what's your next move, Dillon?" Peggy asked.

"Dunno."

"But you're going to leave? You are, aren't you?"

"Well, yes... obviously. One day."

"But I can tell you're thinking about it – about leaving soon, that is."

"What makes you say that?"

"I can just tell, Dillon. Your mood, maybe."

"Actually, I've been offered a position on a national newspaper in London. I haven't had an opportunity like that for a long, long time. It's a great job."

"So you'll go?"

"I'll have to, Peggy. And, truth be told, it's what I've been hoping for. It's what I want. It's what I do."

Jenkins took another sip of tea to reassure himself. He looked up into Peggy Smyth's eyes. They were so large, so bright. And they were looking right at him, sparkling and large and alert to his every word.

Jenkins had taken to leaving the island whenever the squabbling with Smyth grew too intense. He would walk the couple of miles into Fellrock and check his flat, collect mail, do some laundry and then drop in on Peggy Smyth on the way back.

"You know, I don't think he could manage being there on his own," Peggy said, whilst busying about the room.

"But maybe that's a good thing. He can't stay there forever."

"He wants to."

"They won't let him."

"Who?"

"The police, the government, any number of people. And he's getting more vulnerable now that interest is waning. And the police want him off the dual carriageway– "

"They'll have trouble."

"I think we all know that, but he's going to get moved on sooner or later. Anyway, I can't see him sitting on the island through the winter."

"Maybe. Oh, I don't know, Dillon. Actually, I need him to get back to work, truth be told. We don't have much of a mortgage here, but we've got bills to pay."

"Tell me about it!"

"I miss him being around the place, too. It's all very well his being down on the ring road – it's not far and it's easy enough for me to pop down during the day – but it gets lonely here at night. I miss him. I get lonely, Dillon."

Peggy's tone had grown softer. She had picked up a picture frame from the dresser and was looking down at the photograph.

"I miss him, Dillon," she said again, sounding mournful, her eyes fixed on the image.

"I'm sure," Jenkins mumbled, watching her gaze at the photo. "Who is that, Peggy?" he asked, gently.

"The photo? Oh... a boy."

"Nephew?"

"My son actually, Dillon."

"What! Where is– "

She shook her head.

"I'm so sorry, Peggy. I didn't– "

"I don't talk about– "

"No, no, of course– "

"Oh, it's ok, Dillon. I probably should talk about him more. It's just so unbearably sad. And it's been hard. First my husband... and then my son."

Peggy turned her face down towards the photo and then hugged the frame tight to her bosom. Jenkins watched as a tear rolled down her nose. It dripped off the tip and onto her hands. Just the one drop.

The tear empowered Jenkins, who stood up, moved towards Peggy and wrapped his arms around her, cushioning her into his chest. His tenderness seemed to uncork something in her. She looked up at Dillon Jenkins locking onto his eyes, tears streaming down her cheeks to cause what little make-up she was wearing to run into snail-like trails.

"I'm sorry," he started to say. But she stopped him by placing a finger on his lips and then startled him with the softest of kisses.

"You are a sweet man," she whispered.

Jenkins kissed her forehead, kissing her three, four, five times in quick succession, and then her cheeks, her ear, her nose. And she found this strange, but didn't stop him. But he stopped when she placed her mouth on his lips.

Their fingers intertwined and hands locked as they pulled one another closer, tighter and paused. Then fingers found zips and buttons, then loosened and undid them as the kissing grew more frantic and uncontrolled. Then stopped. Suddenly. They broke away, stepping back and looking at each other; her tears subsiding. She smiled, then laughed – laughed loudly, wiping away the teardrops with her sleeve and then her fingers.

Jenkins stood, waiting.

"Shall we?" she asked, quietly.

He offered a gentle smile.

"Why not?" she added after a few seconds, giggling encouragement.

Then her expression changed – calmer and more relaxed.

She turned her back on him and walked away towards the stairs, still clutching the photo in one hand whilst unbuttoning her shirt with the other. He stood for a moment watching her walk, the roll of her hips, before following her up the stairs and then into the bedroom to the right, where she was already sitting on the bed, the photo frame beside her. Her hands were raised behind her head, unfixing her bra. He noticed she was cold. Her pale skin was goose pimply and wrinkled across her stomach, the contours exaggerated by the coldness. He would warm her – make her flesh warm and taut.

He sat down beside her, picking up the frame and looking at the photo.

"What was his name?"

As he asked the question he saw that she was naked. Jenkins let the frame slip onto the floor and leaned forward pressing his chest down onto her breasts, whilst kissing her neck and shoulders.

"He's called Colin, Colin Downey. He was ten," she said in a whisper.

"Downey?"

"My married name."

"What happened?" Jenkins asked between kisses.

"A shooting."

Jenkins sat up abruptly and turned away. He remembered the name.

"I'm so, so sorry."

She reached out, placed a hand around his wrist and pulled him down onto her again, kissing him wildly, whilst helping him to shed the rest of his clothing with nimble fingers.

When Jenkins awoke, he rolled over looking for Peggy Smyth. She had curled up into a tight ball facing out towards the far edge of the mattress. Without making much noise, Jenkins slid from under the covers and stood beside the bed looking for his clothes.

"Stay," she murmured sleepily, "I'll make you breakfast."

"I have to go, Peggy. It's five o'clock in the afternoon."

"Can't be."

"'Tis. You've been sleeping."

"All this time?"

"Look, I'll come back soon. We'll talk, eh?"

"Soon?"

"Very soon."

Jenkins sat on the bed fastening his shirt, leaned over and kissed her on her forehead.

"'Bye now..."

But she was asleep again.

As Jenkins got to his feet, he picked up the photo of Colin Downey. He recognised the face – so young, so innocent – remembering the photographs in the papers at the time of the shooting. There had been so many shootings, and now, so many blurred memories of faces made famous for a moment by the slaughter.

Jenkins put the photograph down on the bedside table, moving a letter lying there out of the way to make room. He was going to fold the letter and tuck it in between the frame and table lamp when the Belfast City Council crest caught his eye.

Dear Mr Craddick, he read, *I am happy to report that at a meeting on 7th September, Belfast City Council voted unanimously to invite your client, Mr Smyth, and his associate, Mr Jenkins, to continue their peace protest on the lawns of Belfast City Hall.*

All the recommendations listed in your proposal have been approved and we are now happy for you to implement the scheme at your earliest convenience.

Please telephone my office early next week to make an appointment. We will then discuss the finer details of what you have in mind...

Jenkins folded the letter and put it back on the bedside table.

30

Thousands had gathered on the streets of Belfast for the official opening of the prefabricated peace island in the grounds of the City Hall. Following weeks of argument, threats and emotional blackmail, Peggy finally convinced Ignatius Smyth that it was time to leave the Ballyblessington ring road. The weather had played its part too – October was incessantly rainy which had made conditions unbearable. Developments in the Peace Process through October had also brought fresh focus to the sit-down protest and Jenkins had managed to convince Smyth that if they did not capitalise on the latest media attention, then an end to their protest might come sooner rather than later. Smyth was also conscious that Jenkins' appearances at the island were growing more fleeting.

An excited crowd stood two and three deep on the pavement opposite the front entrance to Belfast City Hall at the top of Donegall Place, where an area had been cordoned off for the installation of the model of the traffic island on the front lawn.

A shroud had been draped over the model, which was due to be unveiled by a television celebrity flown in from England. PR people fussed about with well-practised smiles, whilst bleached-blonde promotional models shivered within close range of the press cameramen who were poised to take snapshots of anyone who looked vaguely 'A'-, 'B'- or 'C'-list. A DJ, hosting a live radio roadshow, was whipping up the crowd's enthusiasm with a quiz and a cardboard box of free T-shirts.

"Get... me... out... of... here..." Smyth moaned to Jenkins under his breath.

"Oh, come on. It's just a bit of fun. It's great publicity."

"For what? For whom? You're campaigning again, Jenkins. And they'd better not be expecting me to say anything."

"They know you don't talk. Don't worry, I'll take care of that."

"I'm sure you will, but tell me, what the hell is that thing?"

"What... that?" Jenkins shrugged, pointing to the enshrouded replica, just as the TV star yanked on a gold rope to unveil it.

"Why, that's the island, of course. Our island. I think it's damn good, don't you? It's very true to life. It's built to scale. It's exactly the same size as the real one. I mean *exactly* the same size. I gave them measurements. It's an exact replica."

"Why bother? It's only a bloody traffic island. What in hell's name is the point?"

"Authenticity is important. People get pretty excited about our island. It's famous. It's becoming a national monument."

"I don't do monuments. Monuments or icons."

"God! You're like an adolescent son!"

"And what the hell is that?" Smyth asked, pointing at a fibre-glass model to one side of the island.

"Ah, that's Dog, of course."

"It's a tarted-up Guide Dogs for the Blind collection box, for God's sake! It's like a bloody theme park here. Look, if I wanted to live like Mickey Mouse, I'd move to bloody Disneyland."

"It's symbolic. Just go with the flow. It'll be all right. At least there are sanitary facilities and food and drink nearby."

"They have those at the Maze Prison and I don't particularly want to live there either."

Jenkins watched Smyth staring aghast at the white plastic model. *God it's tacky!* he thought, but still hoped that it might help.

Jenkins had liked the model when he was shown rough sketches, then the design drawings and then the photos. He'd been conned into liking the idea by being seduced into contributing to the creative process, but now, as he stood before it with Smyth, he could see how crass the whole concept had been. He felt his cheeks burning red for the first time in a long time.

The prefabricated island sat on the lawns like an enormous fried egg, bright, white and reflecting the sun to a degree that made it hard to look at for any length of time without shielding the eyes. Its only authentic feature was its bollard – the genuine article, as donated by the Roads Service of Northern Ireland. They had hundreds of the things.

Jenkins' main concern was to steer Smyth through the opening ceremony. He didn't like to dwell on the subject of Smyth's lack of enthusiasm, but Jenkins' palms were sweaty with the stress of knowing that things could unravel badly if Smyth wasn't handled well. There were plenty of people in close proximity that he knew would make Smyth uncomfortable and who would also feel it their place to try and engage him in small talk.

Dazzled by the sunlight reflecting off the island, Jenkins spun round to survey the crowd. A spontaneous cheer went up when Jenkins – easily recognisable as one of the Fellrock Two – raised an arm in salute. Buoyed by the crowd's enthusiasm he wondered how much easier things might have been if he had taken control of the peace protest from the start.

"Ok. What do you want me to do, Dillon?"

"It's easy, Iggy. We'll sit it out tonight through to the morning and then if you're still not happy we'll piss off back to Fellrock at the earliest opportunity. If you really don't want to do this, I'll get you a taxi back right now. I can handle this myself. I mean, if you don't want to stay. But do. They're going to lay on a bit of entertainment... a bit of food... a bit of music... people on stilts... jugglers... you know... that kind of thing. It'll be fun. I mean... anyway... you know as well as I do, that we have to do this."

Smyth nodded. It was a tiny movement, but it took Jenkins by surprise; it was almost submissive. Jenkins wondered if Smyth was losing the will to fight.

"You ok, Smyth?"

There came another tiny, almost imperceptible nod, then more silence.

"Shall we get on with it, then?" Smyth mumbled, sloping off in the direction of the plastic island.

31

When Jenkins woke up outside the City Hall the next morning it was still dark with a wintry dankness in the air that, despite the warmth of his sleeping bag, had permeated through to leave him shivering; his teeth chattered.

Dawn in Belfast on that Sunday was spectacular. The city was deserted, giving it a science fiction 'everybody's-been-eaten-alive-murdered-or-kidnapped-by-aliens' quality. Eerie. But Jenkins liked the quiet. And it was very much quieter than the ring road.

Though the sun was yet to fully rise, the street lights were bright enough to illuminate the grounds of the City Hall. The traffic island sat in the middle of one of the widest lawns and was surrounded by the flotsam and jetsam of the night's partying, peppering the sea of green with speckles of brown and white cardboard. There were many bottles.

Jenkins rolled over to look for Smyth. No sign. He then fumbled in his sleeping bag for the flask of tea he had been handed the day before and emptied what was left into the aluminium cup. The tea was tepid and tasted of metal. A couple of sips and Jenkins threw the remainder away. He wriggled out of his sleeping bag and ambled over to the nearest hedge for a pee.

It was then that he spotted a piece of folded notepaper flapping in the mouth of the Guide Dogs for the Blind collection box. He could make out his name handwritten in block capitals on top. Jenkins prised the note from the dog's jaws and held it up under the light of a street lamp whilst screwing up his eyes to bring focus to the scrawled handwriting. The note was signed by Smyth.

Dillon,

I am sorry not to have told you this face-to-face, but presumed that you would try and talk me out of it if I did. You see, I've decided to escape. Yes! I'm leaving the island. I'm standing up and I am going.

As I was saying, I am sorry not to have told you to your face, but you are so persuasive, I am sure you would have found a way of talking me out of it. Anyway I've gone and it's over.

We have a peace process – well pretty much so – and so I think it's time I found something else to do.

I know you won't believe me for a minute if I say that I will miss you, but I will.

Please give me time to regain my balance (or completely lose the plot), then maybe we can meet up in Fellrock and swap stories. Peace be with you... and go home!

Yours, as ever, Iggy.

Gone? Smyth's gone! Jenkins could barely believe it. He scrunched the piece of paper up into a ball and hurled it at the nearest bin, cringing when it clipped the rim and bounced off onto the path below.

So much for the global peace campaign, he thought. Smyth was going home.

It was what Jenkins had wanted from the first, but now he had got his way he felt deflated. It was an empty feeling that reminded him of bedtime on Christmas Days past, climbing the stairs burdened with the sad reality that it was all over for another year.

Jenkins fought with his trench coat to retrieve his portable phone from one of the side pockets. It was charged. Jenkins found British Midland in the address book and dialled.

"Hello. Yes. I want to check the availability of flights from Belfast to Heathrow. Today please. Yes, I'll hold. Thank you."

32

10am, Wednesday 16th April 1997. London.

Jenkins sat semi-conscious in front of his computer screen, his eyes entranced by the cursor winking at him from the top left corner, daring him to tap in a word.

Starting was a step into the dark with a lack of confidence, encumbered with the knowledge that the first paragraph would probably be the worst, have to be rewritten and/or dumped before the day's piece would be fit to go for subbing. Jenkins knew he should limber up with some auto-writing or a sketched outline first, but could never be doing with practice or runthroughs. Taking a deep breath, he typed in a sentence; relieved that he had got under way.

Returning to London and the news department at the *Mail* had been like awakening from a long dream. It was a familiar reality, offering comfort and security. His time in Northern Ireland seemed distant now.

Three years on and his celebrity had dimmed. For months fame stuck to him like a cellophane wrapper that is plucked from hand to hand, finger to finger and still can't be shaken off. But slowly the static charge of his story had waned, and – as with all news – he had become old news. There was nothing remarkable about Dillon Jenkins' personality that kept him to the fore or would make him newsworthy again, and he was relieved to know it. It was achievement enough for him to be back in a reasonable job with good pay and security. He relished the silence of obscurity.

Jenkins still enjoyed occasional celebrity. Whenever the flood waters of political violence rose in Northern Ireland, he would be among the first to be contacted for a comment. By now, however, there were real signs that those flood waters were receding. There was confidence in Westminster and Dublin that the Peace Process would bear fruit. All sides looked set to sit together and talk.

The first lines of Jenkins' article flickered across the screen. It was his spin on the forthcoming general election and the implications for Northern Ireland. Witty observation, backed by hard fact. A challenging and personal preview.

Jenkins was mastering political commentary. It was a pay-off for the time spent on the island. He had graduated from the features department, which fed on a diet of the eccentric and freakish, and was now a columnist; often the *Mail's* commentator on Irish affairs. Jenkins was encouraged to be a voice, was encouraged to ruffle feathers. The responsibility to use his experience to good effect weighed heavily, however. It was a responsibility that often had him staring at a blank screen spellbound by the cursor. It cramped his finger joints and addled his brain.

There also came a haunting inner voice upbraiding him for every lazy metaphor or inaccurate opinion. It argued with him daily, was opinionated and domineering, scrutinising every syllable Jenkins punched into the keyboard. The words were always Jenkins' but the voice was often Smyth's.

Jenkins' column was consistently informative, professional and well-received – but often unremarkable. Jenkins chose it to be so. He liked to keep his head down – well down below the parapet. This was lazy, he knew, but felt he had deserved his place in the sun.

It suited Jenkins to work from a desk at the offices of the *Mail*. He could have filed his copy from his apartment, but preferred the pressure of the office and doubted whether he would find the motivation to work amidst the comforts of home. Not that his flat was that comfortable. He couldn't be doing with too much comfort. Comfortable homes were for the housebound. He agreed with the writer, Quentin Crisp, who observed that once the dust in his bedsit reached a certain depth, it never got any deeper – so why bother to clean it at all? Why waste time with housework when you can be enjoying the outdoor life, the nightlife, that living in a slum encourages?

"Many have given their lives to establish the right of the next generation of Northern Irish citizens to a vote in the coming general election..." Jenkins typed.

"For the Catholics among them, some may only be the second or third generation from their community to be able to do so. And yet, like their English, Scottish and Welsh cousins, it is unlikely that a majority will cast their vote, such is the level of disenchantment felt for our political system amongst the young..."

Jenkins paused and reread the opening two paragraphs. Another day. Another article.

"Look, Gerry, do you really think that that's necessary?"

"No it's not, Dillon, but you're the one that he wants to talk to. Look, the truth is that we might want to lead on this, and we don't know if he'll play ball if you don't go in person."

Jenkins' editor had a talent for man management. He needed Jenkins to do the interview in Belfast and he knew how to coax him into going. Jenkins had to go. The unionist party leader wouldn't talk to anyone else.

"You know if I turn up, it could create a sideshow, Gerry. I don't think that will help our coverage."

"It'll give the story an angle, Dillon. Look, you've got to go back sometime. What's wrong with now? You can be there and back in a day. Do it for *me*, Dillon. Come on man."

"You know I don't want to go, Gerry, don't you? I don't *have* to go."

"Fine, that's ok, Dillon. I'll send Davidson, then. It's about time he cut his teeth on– "

"God, you're a bastard, Gerry!"

"You'll go?"

"If I have to."

"See? You're more competitive than you think, Dillon."

The flight to Belfast was brief, just over the hour, but Jenkins had done it so often the one hour seemed to drag on for two or three. But he was well-used to boredom. He could cope.

Through the window on a clear day the view could be spectacular; Snowdonia, Anglesey, the Isle of Man. This time there was low cloud. It was like night flying, and jerky. And like many old hands, the familiarity with the experience of air travel had bred contempt: with every bump and roll, a lump went to Jenkins' throat. He kept his seat belt on throughout the flight, shut his eyes and thought of Peggy Smyth. She troubled him and weighed on his conscience. He imagined that she would be feeling hard done by by him. He had moved away without hesitation once the protest was over. As soon as an offer of work came from London, he had left Northern Ireland almost immediately. He had suggested to her that she should go with him, but hadn't insisted, hadn't forced the issue, presuming that it would take a lot of persuasion to uproot her. Then he had reassured her that he would be back to stay at weekends and that she could come and visit him in London. Hollow words. And now, sitting in the plane back to Belfast with an opportunity of seeing her, he felt guilty and regretful for he knew hers was a house call he wouldn't be making.

He not only regretted the lack of effort to persuade Peggy to leave Fellrock, but also the lack of confidence that made it easier for him not to try harder. But he realised that he had been afraid. Afraid of the commitment. Afraid of the responsibility of bringing her to London, away from all that she had known, in the knowledge of the hard times she had had in the past. It wasn't that he didn't want the commitment, he knew, but rather that he feared failing her. He didn't dare let her down and contribute another dark chapter to an already black history.

So he had lost her. But what hadn't registered before, and was only dawning on him now, was that *she* had also lost *him*. She had lost another man and it was his fault. He had failed her because he had never given her a chance. He hadn't had the guts to back himself.

And then the plane was descending into Aldergrove, north-west of Belfast – the view across Lough Neagh appearing when they were a couple of hundred feet or so above the runway. Once landed Jenkins pulled his collar up, put his head down and edged his way into the mêlée of people shuffling down and then charging off the plane.

"Ah, Mr Jenkins. Glad you could come. We haven't seen you in these parts for– "

"–a good while. Yeah, I know," Jenkins said, interrupting the unionist party's press officer tersely.

Jenkins was to meet 'the big man', the unionist leader, at a constituency office in Newtownards, County Down. The leader had started soapboxing early in the campaign; it was what he did best. Five minutes late, Jenkins was taken straight through to a back room before he had a chance for a final read-through of his notes and questions. Following a briefing from the press officer, he just had time to change the batteries in his tape machine before being led in to meet his notorious subject.

The interview was done and dusted within twenty minutes. Dillon Jenkins had no idea whether it had gone well or not. The meeting had been much shorter than he expected. The party leader had fed Jenkins the lines he wanted to see reproduced in print and evaded Jenkins' most loaded questions.

Damn! he's given me the slip again, Jenkins thought, as he passed back through reception. But he knew he would be able to flesh out something from his notes and tape. He had easily spotted the soundbites that the leader had been repeating like a mantra and that his party hoped Jenkins would put straight into print. For once the party dogma hadn't been too extreme, but Jenkins would edit it all the same.

The old guy must be mellowing, Jenkins mumbled as he made his way back onto the street. He had expected lunch with the press officer, but with ten days to go until Election Day, lunch was cancelled. Jenkins had a couple of hours to kill before his plane. He was tempted to visit his former colleagues at the *Telegraph* and boast about his new position at the *Mail*, but decided he'd rather go straight back to the airport and start typing the interview onto his laptop whilst it was still fresh in his mind.

A taxi was already waiting for him across the road, the driver leaning against the driver's door having a smoke. He smiled when Jenkins made eye contact.

An amiable driver. *Shit! Why were they always so damn friendly in the North?* Jenkins felt guilty when he chose to sit in the back of the car rather than sit in the front and talk. At least the driver hadn't recognised him.

"Aldergrove, son?"

Jenkins grinned at being considered young enough to be the man's 'son'.

"Yeah. Plenty of time, mate," Jenkins mumbled, trying to appear surly and not the sort to banter.

The driver read his expression and popped on the radio. A talk-in show, *Talkback* with David Dunseith. There was a fierce debate ensuing on the decommissioning of terrorist arms. The discussion was boiling over into a slanging match.

"And we're supposed to trust them? They're effing murderers with blood on their hands. They must think we're mad!" a caller shouted.

"Err... there's a diversion around the town. We'll have to follow this detour. What time's your flight? You ok for time?"

"Yeah. No problem. The flight's not till four-thirty. No rush," Jenkins said. He swallowed hard, seeing the direction that the diversion was taking them.

The weather had been benign since his arrival in the morning. Grey but dry. The long residential road the taxi was diverted onto was almost unrecognisable whilst camouflaged in election posters. One in particular caught Jenkins' attention and made the hair on the back of his neck bristle: 'Vote Martin McGowan – VUP' – and there was the man himself, pinstriped, hair gelled back and beaming godliness behind a 'thumbs up' fist from which the word 'hate' had been carefully airbrushed.

Some peace process, Jenkins thought.

As the taxi approached the junction leading onto the Ballyblessington ring road, Jenkins' brow creased with lines; the surroundings provoking uncomfortable memories.

It was two o'clock. Jenkins could tell by the traffic flow, recognising the afternoon lull that came before the start of the school pick-up run.

"Could you turn left please, mate?"

"You know that'll take us away from the airport?" the driver queried.

"Just a short detour. Won't take a minute. Well, if you've got time that is?"

"Don't worry about that son, as long as you pay the fare."

"Could you take me up to and round the next roundabout – the Fellrock junction – and then we'll turn back towards the airport?"

"No problem, son. Mind you I could show you some prettier landmarks."

They took the bend at the top of the hill and headed down towards the roundabout and the turn-off for Fellrock, which quickly came into view. Jenkins noticed that the grass on the roundabout had grown back thick and lush.

It was anti-climactic to come upon the roundabout and find it so quiet. Strange, Jenkins thought, how their small gathering had at one time attracted TV crews from as far away as Japan and Australia.

He leaned his head back onto the headrest, blew out his cheeks and closed his eyes. Nostalgia was a potent emotion. What had they achieved, anyway? Maybe nothing.

As the taxi swung past the traffic island at the top of the Fellrock road, Jenkins rolled his head towards the window to take a last look.

"Hey, would you go round one more time, please?" Jenkins asked, suddenly sitting upright and leaning forward.

"What? The roundabout?"

The driver turned down his radio.

"Yeah. I think I saw something."

"I doubt it, son. You needed to be here a couple of years ago. We had all sorts going on, then. There were crowds of people hanging around here in those days."

"Yeah? Never mind. One last lap, eh?" Jenkins sighed.

They were already halfway round.

"Stop, stop! Please pull over. Over there! There, by the turn-off. Yes, this'll do, thanks."

The driver looked at Jenkins suspiciously in his mirror as if he thought he might do a runner. Jenkins climbed out of the car and stumbled over to the figure in blue overalls slumped at the foot of the bollard.

"What the hell are you doing here?" Jenkins shouted.

No answer.

"Smyth?"

No answer.

"Smyth, are you drunk?"

Still no answer.

Smyth's eyes were half shut, his hair dirty and matted. He looked jaundiced – his limbs emaciated. Jenkins stooped down and pulled Smyth into a sitting position by his lapels, shaking him to try and bring him round and gain his attention.

"What are you doing here? Are you drunk?" Jenkins asked

again, taking account of the empty bottles strewn around the bollard.

"Of course I'm bloody drunk. I've been drinking. That's what happens. Yeah, Behan said that."

"Who?"

"Brendan Behan. Wrote 'Borstal Boy'."

"And?"

"Don't you know the story?"

"What story?"

"Behan. Guinness once asked him to write an advertising slogan. He said he would need a crate of Guinness, a sizeable fee and a room in the Shelbourne Hotel. They were keen. They agreed. So, Behan in bedroom, executives pacing the corridor and all they can hear is Behan crashing about the room and the chink of glass. They wait and they wait. Finally, there's silence. Tentatively they let themselves in. And what do they find?"

"What?"

"An empty crate of Guinness, Behan lying asleep on the floor surrounded by beer bottles and a handwritten note on the table."

"And?"

"And what?"

"What did the note say?"

"It was his slogan."

"What did it say?"

"*Guinness makes you drunk.*"

"Yes, very funny," Jenkins said, frowning and lighting a fag. "Anyway, what the hell *are* you doing here, Smyth?"

"It's what tramps do."

"But you're not a bloody tramp."

"Actually, I've been practising for years and now I think I've finally cracked it."

"You're just drunk, man."

"Naturally. It's a prereq... a prereq... it's part of the job description."

"What? What am I supposed to say? What do I do?" Jenkins asked, getting angry.

"Nothing. You don't have to say or do anything. Just go. Just go away."

"But, what can I do?"

"Nothing," Smyth said, slumping back into a foetal position.

"But what are– "

"Peace and quiet," he mumbled. "I just come here for some peace and quiet. Ok?"

"Ok, ok, I get the message. Look if you need anything– "

"Yeah, I'll light a fire and send up lots of smoke."

"But plenty of smoke, now."

"Sure. Plenty of smoke," Smyth said, yawning and then falling into a doze which commenced with a deep sigh and a loud snore.

Jenkins got to his feet and turned towards the taxi.

"Is he all right?" the driver yelled through his open window.

"Yeah. I guess so," Jenkins said, shrugging and then climbing into the back.

"Hey, isn't that that man Smyth? Smyth the– "

"Ignatius Smyth? No. Looks like him, but no."

The taxi driver muttered something Jenkins couldn't decipher then switched the radio back on.

As the taxi moved off, Jenkins twisted round to look out of the rear window. He stared at the view of Smyth shrinking in the glass and just in time to see the dog emerging from the trees beyond the roundabout and limping over towards the island.

33

It was three months after Jenkins' trip to Belfast that he heard the news. Peggy called him late one night. Ignatius had been complaining of a pain in his stomach, she said, and for a long time, wouldn't go and see the local GP. But then the pain had become severe. The GP referred him to a specialist for some extensive prodding. The specialist made no effort to disguise the severity of the test results.

"Let's get to the point. The prognosis isn't good I'm afraid, Mr Smyth. The cancer has been vigorous – has spread rapidly. I'm afraid we've detected some cancerous cells in your liver."

"How long?"

"Weeks, maybe a month or two. Three at the most."

A month later, Smyth was admitted to a hospice. Going into month two, he summoned Jenkins.

The hospice was located high on the Antrim Road with views down Belfast Lough towards Scotland and the Ayrshire coast. It was a large detached building, Victorian and Gothic, and whilst it had once housed a wealthy industrialist and his family of five, it was now home to around thirty-five terminally ill patients, many of whom were suffering from cancer. It was a rambling four-storey house with carved wooden eaves. Jenkins imagined that it must have looked pretty grand in its heyday, but was now diminished by generations of cheap paint jobs and the addition of concrete ramps, a cast iron fire escape and thin splashes of tarmac – potholed where the weeds were creeping back.

"Thank God you're here," Peggy Smyth said, grasping Jenkins by the hand and then hugging him as he stepped into the foyer. She was on her way home. "He's not great, but he's comfortable. He's been asking for you, Dillon," she continued.

"I'm so glad I could come. And I'm so sorr– "

"Don't be. It doesn't help. Anyway, it's such a pity that there's so little they can do except make him comfortable and feed him the right drugs. Brace yourself before you go in now, Dillon. And don't be looking shocked when you see him. It would upset him, you know. And no tears. Pease don't cry."

Peggy had been fixing him with a serious expression. He was relieved when she broke into a smile. She touched his arm.

"Please come by the house when you're through, Dillon."

"'Course," Jenkins said, then leaned down to kiss her on the cheek. For a moment they looked into each other's eyes, just long enough to make Jenkins wonder if there was still a chance.

"We'll talk, Peggy. I've missed you, you know."

"I hope so," she said quietly, before turning to go.

At the top of the hall she paused and looked round: "I've missed you too," she said softly, smiling again.

He watched the sway of her hips till she turned a corner heading for the car park and wondered.

Jenkins was relieved to find that Smyth's room was at least clean. The scent of disinfectant was a stark reminder of the business at hand though, and barely masked the lingering scent of decay.

The room's decor was pleasant enough. He wouldn't mind remembering the scene. Smyth was propped up on a pile of pillows. There was a broad view of the lough from his bed.

"What the hell are you doing in here Smyth, you lazy bastard?"

"Ah, Englishman. Come to annoy me, huh?" Smyth croaked. His mouth looked parched, his lips chapped and the skin bruised where a tube had been clipped.

Jenkins smiled. He had had enough time to imagine the worst, but thankfully the reality wasn't quite as grim as the picture he had conjured up.

Smyth was being attended to by a male nurse, replenishing the drip attached to Smyth's arm. The arm was emaciated; skin and bone. It must have been difficult for the nurse to find a vein.

'Withered' was Jenkins' first impression of Smyth: too thin and very frail. Like a doll a small child could lift in one hand. His skin was the colour of porcelain, but with the texture of dried fruit.

"Would you rather I come back and do this in a wee while?" the nurse enquired.

"Please don't go on my account," Jenkins urged.

"Mr Jenkins won't be staying here long, Nurse. I can't stand his company for more than about five minutes at a time," Smyth croaked in a hoarse whisper. "Anyway, Mr Jenkins is a busy man these days," he continued, his mouth cracking into a smile which made the chaps blink.

"I'll come back when you two've finished. This can wait a while," the male nurse insisted.

The nurse shuffled round the bed and then limped out of the room supporting himself with a cane: rocking from side to side as if his hips and knees were cast in rusty iron. He dragged the door shut behind him; then silence.

Jenkins sat down and waited for a moment, glancing out of the window at the view and wishing he could have a smoke.

"Glad you came."

"Of course."

"No, *I'm* glad *you* came, you *eejit*, Dillon. Anyway, what have you been up to?"

"Writing. The usual crap, you know. And you?"

"I've been ill and dying."

"Nice one. How's it going?"

"Looks like I'm going to get it right first time."

"Congratulations."

"Got any fags?"

"I didn't think you smoked."

"I was thinking of taking it up."

"Cigarettes kill, you know."

"Bastards."

"Anyway why the hell would you want to smoke, for God's sake, Iggy?"

"Smoking cures kippers?"

"Ha bloody ha."

"Seriously... can you get me out of here, Dillon?"

"Looks like you'll be checking out of here quite soon, anyway."

"Yes, but I want to leave on my feet, not feet first."

"You joking?"

"Do I look like I'm joking? Look, I'd rather you took me out of here, laid me on the side of a hill and ran me through with a bayonet than left me to die in this place."

"You sure?"

"Absolutely. Look, I want you to get me out of here, ASAP."

"Ok. But where do you want to go?"

"You know where."

"Look. You can't go there, you idiot."

"Maybe, maybe not. But I really, really need to get out of here. I might even consider going home. By the looks of things it won't be for long and the nurse'll kit me out with all the drugs needed to keep me quiet."

"Ok. When?"

"Come back tomorrow. I'll get Peggy to sort it at this end."

As he left the hospice and headed for the car park, Jenkins put a cigarette to his lips, then patted his pockets for matches.

"Want a light?"

Smyth's nurse was sitting on the bottom steps of the fire escape at the side of the building.

"Oh, thanks."

Jenkins strolled over and cupped his hands round the male nurse's lighter and took a deep drag. As he took the flame Jenkins glanced up into the nurse's eyes. There was an intensity to his stare, yet a lack of focus which masked expression; a blackness that was cold and haunting. However his general demeanour was gentle; he exuded a reassuring professionalism.

"Just having a quick one myself," the nurse said, now smiling.

"Thanks. And thanks for taking care of my friend."

"No problem... though he seems happier when the Italian nurse comes in after lunch."

"Italian, hey? He has an eye for Latin ladies."

"Seems so."

"A demanding job, though?" Jenkins asked, taking another drag and avoiding eye contact.

"It's not always easy, but it has its rewards, you know. Most of the people we get in here are quite inspirational. I've met some very brave people here. Your friend is a case in point."

"How is he?"

"He's comfortable and his spirits are fine. There are times when he still thinks he can beat the cancer, but then many of our patients do."

"It gets them in the end, though?"

"Well, this is the last stop for many, but we've had the odd exception."

"Doesn't the attrition rate get you down?" Jenkins asked in a lowered voice.

"That we lose so many? Of course. But that's the job – to make people as comfortable as we can under the circumstances. And, when the time comes, help them die with dignity."

"More power to you."

"Err, your friend, Mr Jenkins... he's a character all right," the male nurse said, taking a final drag and then stamping on the stub. "Funnily enough, I knew him before he came here, you know. You might say we were pretty close at one time. I knew you too... well, from a distance."

"Oh?"

Jenkins felt uncomfortable.

"You know, from the protest."

"Were you there?"

"Kind of. Briefly."

"Seems a lifetime ago, now. A bit of a waste of time really."

"Really?"

"Perhaps. I don't know. Maybe. I don't think our efforts made much difference in the long run. Not that that really matters. Anyway... what's your name, sir?"

"You won't have heard of me."

"Try me."

"Tommy."

"Tommy what?"

"Thomas McShane."

"Nice to meet you, Thomas."

They shook hands, McShane lit another cigarette and the two smoked on in silence.

33

4.00am, Thursday 16th October, 1997. Fellrock, County Down.

Twilight. Crows tapped on the roof of Peggy Smyth's cottage. Peggy heard the drumming and looked up. There was nothing to see but the blank canvas of the ceiling. Looking around the kitchen filled her with sadness; a regret that what she was about to do hadn't been done many years before.

The kitchen was bare, as was the lounge and the hall and stairs, and, upstairs, the bathroom and two smallish bedrooms. Stripped bare the cottage smelt musty – quite lifeless save for the tapping of the crows. Everywhere dust and sunlight had left outlines of possessions now packed away.

And she was glad to be leaving.

Above the noise of the birds' pecking a sudden knock made her jump. The front door. Time to go.

Peggy lifted her brown suitcase, looked around the hall one last time, blinking as if to take a mental snapshot and then slowly opened the front door.

"Hello, Peggy."

"You didn't make the funeral, then?"

"No."

Dillon Jenkins had been anticipating the reproach and had prepared his simple response well in advance.

"Is that it, Dillon?"

"Yes," he replied without facial expression and in the assertive manner he had rehearsed.

"Are we all right for time?"

"Absolutely, Peggy. The flight's at nine, we'll be at the airport by seven."

Dillon Jenkins escorted her to the hire car, relieved her of her case and ushered her into the front.

As soon as the car moved off she felt the past falling away like a dead skin.

"It'll be ok, Dillon, won't it?"

"Safest way to travel."

"No. I mean London."

"We'll be fine."

"What if it doesn't work out?"

"Then we'll come back here. We can get the roof fixed."

"That's not what I meant."

"I know, Peggy..." Jenkins said, smiling with new-found confidence.

As they came over the Craigantlet Hills they caught a glimpse of the SeaCat ferry ploughing down Belfast Lough, heading for Scotland. Above, seagulls hung on the air struggling to beat the head wind, whilst on the horizon a tatty bulk carrier was approaching, covering the last few miles into Belfast harbour at a crawl. From the car it was impossible to spot the figure on the foredeck, swinging a five-wood and firing golf balls out to sea into the last of the daylight.